death on sacred ground

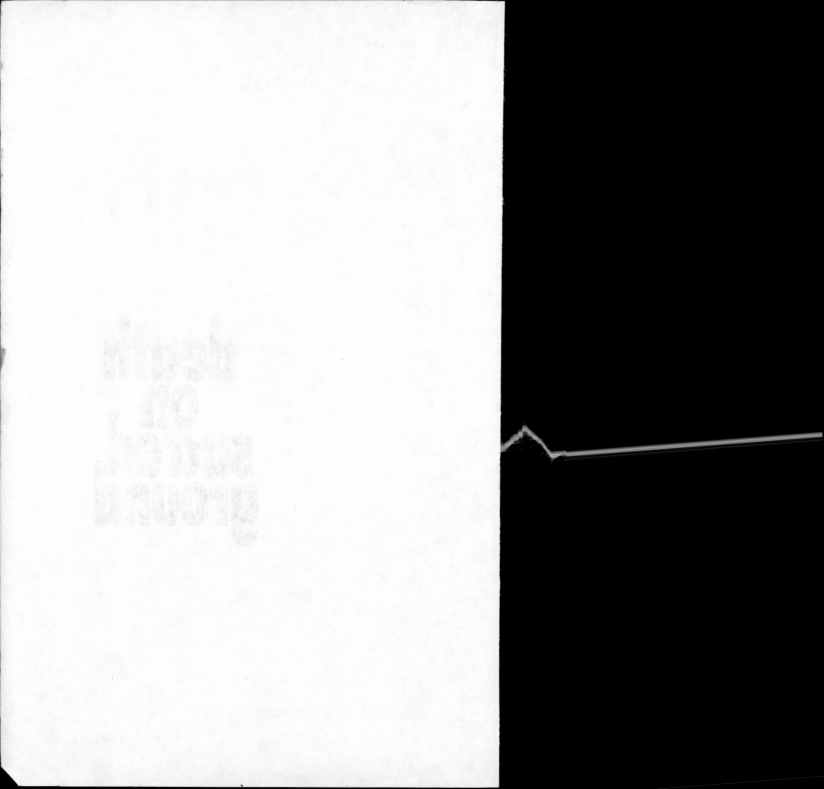

death on sacred ground

Harriet K. Feder

Lerner Publications Company ■ Minneapolis

My thanks to DuWayne "Duce" Bowen of the Seneca Nation of Indians, author and staff member of the Seneca-Iroquois National Museum at Salamanca, New York, for his insights into the Kinuza Crisis; to those museum staffers for their informative exhibits and publications; to my editors Martha Brennecke and Katy Holmgren, whose invaluable assistance helped make all the bits and pieces come together; to the Right Writers of Buffalo, N.Y., for their constructive critiquing of my story, and as always to my husband, Herbert Feder, for trekking along on the research trail, resolving computer crises, reading the manuscript, and being there for me.

Lerner Publications Company
A division of Lerner Publishing Group
241 First Avenue North
Minneapolis, MN 55401 U.S.A.

Website address: www.lernerbooks.com

Library of Congress Cataloging-in-Publication Data

Feder, Harriet K.
    Death on Sacred Ground: a Vivi Hartman adventure / by Harriet K. Feder
        p.   cm.
    Summary: When tenth grader Vivi Hartman arrives with her rabbi father at a Seneca reservation to arrange the funeral of a Jewish girl who died violently, she finds herself investigating rumors of murder.
    ISBN 0-8225-0741-2
    [1. Murder—Fiction. 2. Jews—United States—Fiction. 3. Seneca Indians—Fiction. 4. Indians of North America—New York (State)—Fiction. 5. Indian Reservations—Fiction. 6. New York (State)—Fiction. 7. Mystery and detective stories.] I. Title.
PZ7.F2995 Mi 2001
[Fic]—dc21   00-009706

Manufactured in the United States of America
1 2 3 4 5 6 – SB – 06 05 04 03 02 01

To Ben, Ari, Michael, Molly, Ilana,
Nyan, and those yet to come.

And Dinah the daughter of Leah, whom she had borne unto Jacob, went out to see the daughters of the land. And Shechem the son of Hamore the Hittite, the prince of the land saw her. . . .

—Genesis XXXIV

sunday

chapter 1

"Pikes Landing?" Rachael yelled.

My face got hot as the other kids at our Sunday school lunch table turned to look at me. Rachael glared at them, then lowered her voice and screwed up her nose.

"Your father is dragging you down to that hick town on the reservation for the whole winter break?"

I swallowed the last of my sandwich. "Just for part of the school vacation, but for the whole week before, too. Dad has to be there to do this funeral, and of course he has to stay for the week of mourning. We leave right after his last class today. But I'm not getting off as easy as you think. He made me call each of my teachers and ask for homework."

Rachael shrugged. "At least you won't have classes like the rest of us."

"That's what I thought. But my social studies teacher had other ideas. Mr. Frank said with all that's going on these days down on the Seneca reservation, it's got to be affecting the kids at the high school."

"So?"

"So because I've shown such interest in the Iroquois, he said, he was sure I would like to do an ethnography."

"A what?"

"Ethnography. They do them a lot in anthropology. You follow a person around to study something about their life. Mr. Frank was so enthusiastic about it, he put through a call to his cousin Mr. Parker, who just happens to be the principal of Pikes Landing Central."

"You're kidding?"

I shook my head. "As far as the school is concerned, it's a fait accompli. Only problem is that they didn't match me with a Seneca. The school paired me off with a townie named Paula Ash instead."

"Great!" Rachael said. "And what about Florida with your grandma? Mike will be down there, won't he? Isn't this winter break for him?"

I nodded.

"And you sit there calmly eating your lunch, when you'll hardly be with your boyfriend on break?" Rachael sighed. "Honestly, Vivi Hartman, sometimes I think having a rabbi father has made you autonomously challenged."

Not that again! I've never been a wimp about women's rights, but Rachael just discovered them this year. Her latest shtick is "women power," and her favorite word is "autonomy," in all of its forms.

"I don't know," I said. "I'll probably make it to Florida by midbreak. Mike and I can be together then. And, for your information, Dad's not taking me. I'm taking him!" I held out a small white card.

"Oh, Vivi! You're using your junior license?"

I smiled. "And I can even drive at night, because we took that driver's ed course."

"I thought your father put the freeze on using that license until next year."

"Right! But when he made that decision, Dad didn't know that he would break an ankle skiing and have this funeral to do in the southern tier of the state."

Rachael nodded. "That would give a person a change of heart."

"Not heart, Rachael, mind. Remember it's my dad we're talking about." My dad's heart is bigger than anyone's, but it's not what he uses for thinking. I glanced down the table and raised my voice just the right amount. "Not only is he letting me use my license, but I get to drive all the way from Buffalo to Pikes Landing."

"Wow! That has to be sixty miles. Some people have all the luck."

I shrugged and dug into my lunch bag. There had to be another cookie.

chapter 2

"Is that all you are taking?" my father nodded at the backpack I had tossed into the
minivan, next to his beat-up valise, Farfel's
kennel, and the kosher groceries he had hur-
riedly ordered for the trip.

"An extra pair of jeans, shirt, a skirt for services, underwear, and running shoes." I looked
at him. "That should be enough. Gram said
there's a washer and dryer, didn't she?"

"Well, not exactly. What she said was, 'the rabbi's
apartment has all the modern conveniences.'"

"Great! No sweat!"

Dad sighed. "Vivi, *yakeerati* (my dear), my
mother last visited Pikes Landing in 1951
when her friend Shirley had a baby."

"Yikes!"

"Exactly." My father looked at the supplies. "Well, I guess that's everything. Shirley assured me that the old temple has two working fireplaces to keep us warm if the power should go out in a winter storm. And I brought more than enough candles for Sabbath and the mourners. We can use the rest for light. If the fridge won't work, we won't have to worry about perishables. We'll just put them out on the ice and pack them with snow." He looked at me. "Where are you going, Vivi?"

"Be back in a minute," I said. "Just want to get some boots and my down parka. And that ski underwear Mom sent me from Switzerland. And maybe my quilt and—"

It wasn't until we were racing along the thruway (well, not exactly racing—Dad made me go ten miles under the speed limit) that he told me more about Shirley.

"She's not just Gram's friend," he said. "She's *mishpacha*, family. A distant cousin on my father's side. I spoke to her on the phone, but I've never met her myself. It seems she has a granddaughter just about your age. Shirley is sure you two will be great friends."

So much for autonomy! I studied the road, which had changed from a boring, flat ribbon to rolling, rocky hills. Bare-branched trees at the crests of the hills were glazed with snow, and the valleys in between looked dry and brown. As I executed a cool S-turn, Farfel, asleep at Dad's feet, yawned and turned over, but Dad's shoulders tensed. The jaw beneath his trim copper beard was as set as the granite cliffs framing the highway. Would he ever have confidence in my driving?

I sighed. "So this granddaughter and I are related?"

Dad nodded. "It would seem so."

"And the old person who died. Was that a relative, too?"

My father's voice got low. "It wasn't an old person, yakeerati. It was a girl about your age."

I tightened my hands on the wheel. People my age were dying all the time, but only in the papers and on TV. No one personally connected to me. Not that this girl was connected exactly, but still. . . .

Dad slapped the dashboard in front of him. "A hunting accident. What kind of Jews go hunting?"

I couldn't think of any that I knew, unless I counted Rachael's brother, Saul. Ever since that day last year when he hit a deer with his car, some of the kids call him "The Great Jewish Hunter." Poor Saul. The police said it wasn't his fault. And it sure wasn't the deer's. With most of their space gone condo and rutting season upon them, they had been running frantically through town. Still, whenever Saul thinks of that beautiful, dead buck, he gets pains in his stomach. Pains like I was having now. I opened the window and gulped breaths of cold, moist air. A girl my own age was dead. Dry, lifeless leaves were blowing across the road.

"Food, souvenirs, and cheap gas: next exit!" Dad read from a billboard. I knew we had entered the Seneca reservation.

My social studies teacher's voice invaded my head. "Gas stations on reservation land don't have to add on taxes to pay to the state. But that probably won't last long," I remembered him saying.

"Why not?" someone had asked.

I remembered how the teacher had grimaced. "Non-Indian gas stations claim it's unfair competition. They're pressuring New York State to pass a law forcing the Indians to pay the same taxes as people do elsewhere."

I frowned. "Guess we'd better get gas before the price goes up, Dad."

My father shook his head. "Don't worry, Vivi. That bill will never pass. Neither the state nor the federal government can make laws on Indian land," he said.

I sniffed. "Smell that smoke? And look, Dad. There are flames up ahead!"

My father's voice tightened. "Turn off at this exit, Vivi. It's a good time to fill up the tank."

"And miss the fire?"

Dad didn't answer. He grabbed the wheel and swerved us onto the shoulder, out of the way of the burning tire whizzing toward us. From a stand of trees beyond the shoulder, two men appeared in front of our minivan.

Shaking, I hit the brake.

Dad's hand came down on the automatic lock on the passenger side. Nothing happened. "I knew I should have gotten this fixed before we left!" he said. "Lock your door, Vivi."

As I did, one of the men raised a sign, "More tax—less road!"

"This is our land!" the man shouted.

"Move slowly, Vivi," Dad said. "Go to the exit and turn right." His voice was low and controlled, the kind that allowed no argument. Carefully, I released the brake.

"These protests can get violent," he said.

I turned onto a narrow two-laner and followed the signs to the gas station. "So the fires divert the traffic off the thruway, and the state loses money from the tolls. Maybe even more than they would gain from the taxes. You have to admit it's a neat idea, Dad."

"Yes, as long as no one gets hurt. Guess we'll take the back road into town. Whoa, slow down. Pull over at that pump in front of the candy and souvenir store."

Suddenly I felt ravenous. "Can I get a candy bar?"

"Later. First fill the tank." He handed me his credit card. I parked the minivan by a pump and hit the tank cover release. Farfel barked and jumped into my seat as I got out and picked up the gas gun.

"Last time I looked, that was my job, lady," a man behind me said. He grabbed the hose from my hand and started fueling. "Hope your husband has cash. Don't take those dang cards."

"He's not my husband!"

"All right then, your boyfriend."

I took a breath. "He's not my boyfriend either. He's my father." The old guy squinted at the passenger seat as Dad lowered the window.

"Hi," he said, "I'm Rabbi Hartman. What do I owe you?"

The man looked at the meter. "Five fifty-six. Cash." He picked up a sponge and wiped down the windshield then tugged at the hood.

"No need for that." Dad said. "I checked the oil before I left."

The man frowned. "Harry Blacksnake don't do half a job."

Dad nodded. "I'm glad to know that," he said. "I have an automatic lock that needs work. I'll bring it in soon. But I'm in a hurry now. I have to conduct a funeral today."

Harry Blacksnake pulled at the hood until it and my father gave. "If you're here for the Solomon girl," Harry said, "they won't be needing you in no hurry, preacher."

My father sighed. "You don't understand. According to our law, the deceased should be buried right away."

"Yeah," Harry said, "that's what Moshé Solomon says. But the police aren't buying it, are they? Paper said they want an autopsy. Around here, that could take days."

Dad grimaced. "An autopsy? For an accident?"

Harry closed the hood and nodded. "Folks around town aren't so sure it was an accident. They're saying that girl was murdered."

chapter 3

Murdered? Neither Dad nor I spoke as we drove toward Pikes Landing. I tried to think of the stories Gram told me about summers at Grandpa's aunt's house on the lake. She'd told me about Main Street with the library, the movie house, the soda fountain inside the drugstore, and my great-uncle's men's clothing store.

The Pikes Landing I drove through didn't have any of them. It had houses with peeling paint and ragged "for sale" signs. Christmas lights dangling limply between two street lamps didn't do much to brighten the scene on Main Street. A woman came out of the corner supermarket, one arm around a paper bag, the other holding her worn coat closed. Two men in iridescent orange hunting jackets went into the corner pub.

"Some things never change," my father said, his eyes on the hunters, "not even with the end of a lease and an era."

I knew he meant the ninety-nine-year land lease. Three years ago, when the lease ended, Pikes Landing had been on the news every day. Everyone had learned how the Seneca had leased the land to the white men for a song, and the white men had built a very prosperous town. Since Pikes Landing was actually reservation land, anyone who lived there or operated a business didn't have to pay property taxes. And one day, poof! The lease was up, and the Seneca raised the rent sky high. High enough to make up for the poverty they had endured while trying to survive on the hunting and planting skills of their old culture.

"The Indians were poor for so long," I said. "No one can blame them for trying to make some profit at last."

My father grimaced. "Unfortunately, a lot of people do, like the ones who had to move because they couldn't afford the new rents on their homes. And the ones whose businesses died for lack of customers. Even some religious folk whose churches had to consolidate to survive. As for the Jews—"

"What, Dad?"

"Some of our people are angry, too. Angry that there aren't enough Jews left in town to support a rabbi or pay for the upkeep of the temple." My father sighed and glanced at the little black book where he writes down just about everything. "Turn left at the next corner, Vivi."

As I made the turn, he pointed to a building set back among large, old trees.

"354 Maple. This is it!"

Temple Beth David was a three-story box of old, red brick. If one could believe the huge glass-enclosed bulletin board on the front lawn, the last scheduled event was a Sukkoth service back in October.

As I shifted into park, a kid came around the side of the building and jogged up the porch steps. At the top of the stairs, she grabbed a broom. Her back toward me, she swept the leaves and snow off the steps, her long red braid swinging pendulum-style down the length of her faded Buffalo Bills sweatshirt.

I opened the window and called, "Hi!"

The girl turned slowly and looked at me, her feet planted warily. Finally, she put down the broom and sidled toward me like a cat approaching a rottweiler. She looked about my age, but she had stopped growing about where my neck started. I held out my hand.

"My name's Aviva Hartman," I said. "I drove

my father down from Buffalo."

She ignored me. Swiping a dead leaf off the leg of her black cords, she walked around to the passenger side and looked up at my father. "Are you the rabbi?"

Dad smiled. "That I am." He looked at her broom. "Hard work after a day at Sunday school."

"There isn't any Sunday school. Hasn't been since the rabbi left last year." She pulled a key from her pants pocket and handed it to him, glaring. "It unlocks both the front and back doors," she said, then turned and started back toward the temple.

"Thanks, Miss—?" Dad called.

The girl kept walking and disappeared behind the building. Seconds later, her red mountain bike whizzed out of the alley, onto the road.

"A hostile kid," Dad said as I helped him out of the car and handed him his crutches.

chapter 4

Gram had remembered right about the two fireplaces. One of them was in the rabbi's study. Since it was the only one on the first floor and my father could not walk the stairs, he would have to use the room both as an office and a bedroom.

In a front room on the second floor, I found the other fireplace. Touching the rough, gray stone of the mantle, I knew I'd be okay if the old furnace went out. There was no doubt that the giant hearth had withstood the worst of storms. It promised to cast a warm glow on the dark wood floor and heavy oak furniture.

Better get some firewood in soon, I thought, watching a flurry of snowflakes begin their ballet outside my window. I set Farfel's kennel before the hearth. As I put a photo of Mike and me on the dresser to mark the room as mine, I heard a loud knock on the kitchen door. Farfel began barking, and I started downstairs but stopped midway since Dad had already opened the door.

"So this is Tessie's boy," a woman said, depositing two large shopping bags on the table. I noticed her slight Hungarian accent, as if she'd come to the United States as a very young child. I'm good at detecting accents, even faint ones. The talent comes from my mom, I guess. She's a linguist who teaches at a big university in France. Shirley Imber brushed some snow off her short, straight gray hair and looked at Dad. "A rabbi. Such a blessing for your dear mother." She led Dad to a chair. "Come, come, sit down, Patrick. Rest your leg. So I've met the dog, but where is that gorgeous daughter of yours?"

Oh, no! Gram had been at work again, pouring on her propaganda. Gorgeous? My best friend, Rachael, can only come up with "interesting" when describing my tall, lanky looks. Mike, my boyfriend, even thinks I'm pretty, although he happens to be partial to unruly brown curls. But "gorgeous" could only come from the lips of a grandmother. I turned to make a stealthy retreat.

Too late! "Here she is now," my father said.

"Come down here, Vivi, and meet our cousin—Shirley Imber."

The woman clasped me to her ample bosom, the top of her head inches below my chin. "So this is little Vivi!" She stepped back, holding me at arm's length to examine me with faded blue eyes. "I can't wait for you to meet Paula, my granddaughter. You two will be great friends." She looked at Dad. "I sent her over this morning to clean up the place. She did a good job?"

"Fine!" my father said.

"I hope so." Shirley Imber looked skeptical. She went to the table and started emptying grocery bags, stocking the fridge and the freezer. "Look, matzo ball soup, chicken, pot roast, and gefilte fish. All homemade. Kosher, from my own kitchen. There's milk and fruit, too—a growing girl should eat good." She looked at my father. "And you also, Patrick. Milk will heal those broken bones." She plunked down a plate of sweet rolls. "You'll have a little tea, no?"

"Thank you, Shirley," Dad said, "but I'm afraid I'll have to take a rain check. I must get over to the Solomon place and see about the funeral." He stood up and reached for his crutches.

Shirley filled the kettle anyway. "You shouldn't be insulted, Patrick, if Moshé seems not too friendly. He would have preferred an Orthodox rabbi."

Dad sat down again. "Moshé Solomon is Orthodox?"

Shirley nodded. "His mother and father didn't raise him that way. They were part of our temple, but. . . . "

"But what?"

"You should have seen him, Patrick. Some kid he was. Never went to school. He drank, took drugs, everything. His poor parents dragged him to all kinds of programs for help. Nothing worked. Finally they sent him to an Orthodox school in Brooklyn." She shook her head. "He was only fifteen. Yet who could blame them?"

"And the Orthodox school turned him around?" Dad asked.

"Oh, yes! And they taught him his own father's trade as well. Made him a match, too. At nineteen, they married him off. They turned him into such a *rebbe*, he has almost nothing to do with the rest of us." She sighed. "If only he had stayed in Brooklyn."

"Why didn't he?" Dad asked.

Shirley bit her lip. "Five months after Moshé left for school, his mother got pneumonia and died. At the funeral, Moshé couldn't stop crying. Some people say it was guilt. But I think he really loved her. When his first daughter was born, he named her Mindel, after his mother, didn't he?" The old woman winced, as if in pain. "Last year, when his father passed away, Moshé suddenly, to everyone's surprise, came here with his family and took over his father's garage himself, just when everyone else seemed to be leaving."

"Did he say why?" Dad asked.

Shirley nodded. "He said things were bad in Brooklyn. He couldn't make a living, so he hoped that things would be better up here. And it seemed as if God was truly with him. With most folks around here poor and driving old cars, the repair business is suddenly booming. Now Moshé is even building a used car lot on that rocky corner property next door."

My father's brow puckered. "Still, an Orthodox family must find life hard in this town. With no Orthodox school, kosher stores, or ritual bath," he said.

Shirley shrugged. "Once a month, the wife goes into Buffalo and comes back with a truckload of kosher food. They have eight kids to feed, God bless them. They home-school the little ones themselves. The two older boys, they sent to Israel to study."

"But the eldest daughter was in the local high school?"

"Yes. She insisted on it. Threatened to run away if her parents didn't let her go." Shirley wiped her eyes. "Believe me, Patrick, Moshé and his wife had misgivings. But such a tragedy they never figured on."

"Poor man. He must be devastated," Dad said. "But why didn't he call an Orthodox rabbi from Brooklyn to do the funeral?"

Shirley looked down at her hands. "I convinced him to let me call you instead."

"But—" began Dad.

"No, wait!" She held up her hand. "Folks around here don't understand our ways, Patrick. They are suspicious about why Moshé wants the funeral so fast. He doesn't even want to wait for his boys to come home. Think about how that looks. They're saying that maybe he killed his own daughter. And now the police want to do an autopsy. With so few of our people left in this town, we don't need this kind of trouble." She looked at Dad, her eyes pleading. "I figured that you being from around these parts, you can speak their language better than a rabbi from Brooklyn. That maybe you could turn the police around."

My father touched her arm. "I doubt it," he said. "Law enforcement has their own job to do." He stood up. "But I'll do what I can for the family. How do I get to Moshé Solomon's house?"

"I'll drive you," Shirley said. "I have some cake to bring to them and the house is only a few blocks from here. But first I have to make a phone call." She walked to the kitchen telephone and dialed. "Paula? You're doing your homework? So what's the TV doing on? Listen, I'm at the temple. I have to drive the rabbi to the Solomon house. Be a good girl and come over and stay with Vivi."

My face got hot. "I don't need a baby-sitter," I said.

Shirley ignored me, her ear to the phone. "So you can work on your history homework here. Maybe Vivi can help you. She's very smart from what I hear."

I winced.

"You'll be at the temple in ten minutes, or you can forget about the movies this weekend, understand?" Shirley said, and she hung up. "Teenagers. I'm too old for them."

"Does Paula live with you?" my father asked.

"Only when my daughter is away on business. Lee is a children's book illustrator. Maybe you've heard of her. Lee Ash?" Shirley set out some napkins and spoons. "So sit down, Patrick. While we're waiting, we might as well have tea. The sweet rolls shouldn't go to waste."

chapter 5

Ash! Paula Ash! My face got hot. Shirley's granddaughter was the girl who had been sweeping snow at the temple. The girl I was supposed to follow around at school for my report.

"A hostile kid," my father had called her.

Hostile? Who wouldn't be hostile if suddenly you're called to the principal's office and told that some kid from Buffalo is going to be on your tail for the next few days? I couldn't blame her at all if she loathed me.

Paula Ash was a girl with autonomy. In spite of her grandmother's threat, she arrived in twenty minutes rather than ten. The snow was falling harder by then. Through the kitchen window, I watched her jump off her bike and park it in the tool shed behind the building. She reached into the basket and grabbed a backpack with a colorful emblem embroidered on it. As she carried it into the back hall, I made out the picture on the patch. Corn, beans, and squash—the staples that had kept the Iroquois alive for centuries. The Iroquois treasured them and called them "the three sisters."

"Neat," I said, pointing to the emblem. "The three sisters." Paula's eyes widened with surprise. Then she quickly looked away, unzipped her parka, and kicked off her running shoes, ignoring Farfel's yips.

"Not exactly Godzilla, is he?"

I bristled. "He may weigh twelve pounds, but he's tough enough when he has to be. And most of all, he's smart."

Paula shrugged and walked into the kitchen. She had changed into jeans and a dark green wool sweater. Her red braid dangled against it like a coiled copper wire, a few wisps escaping to touch her cheeks. Her grandmother tucked them back into place as she kissed her. "Paula, darling, I want you to meet Rabbi Hartman and his daughter, Vivi."

"Hi," the girl said, as if she had never seen us before.

"Hi," I answered. Dad didn't crimp her act either.

"Well, Vivi, isn't this nice company for you?" he said and smiled.

"You'll have some tea, Paula," Shirley said, "then you and Vivi will wash up these few dishes like good girls, yes? Remember, it's strictly kosher here, like in my house. We don't mix dairy with meat. We had milk with our tea, so I served on the dairy dishes. You'll put them away in the dairy cupboard, you hear?" She and my father got their coats. Dad had already opened the door when Shirley came back.

"And don't use the dishwasher. Machines don't do a good job like by hand." As the door closed behind them, I broke up laughing. Paula raised her eyes to heaven and shook her head. She opened the dishwasher to the left of the sink.

"This is the one for the dairy dishes," she said. When we'd loaded the last of the tea things, Paula tossed her backpack on the table and took out a notebook and a history textbook. I watched her open the textbook and turn the notebook to a used page. For a moment, she stood back and looked at the scene as if studying the effect. Then she plopped down a ballpoint and walked away.

"I couldn't care less about history or anything else in that dumb school," she said as I followed her into the sitting room. "If not for you, I'd skip tomorrow for sure. What grade are you in, anyway?"

"Ten," I answered.

"Yeah, me too." She studied me for a moment, then lowered her voice. "I need to talk to your father," she said. "Do you think it's possible?"

"Of course. Just make an appointment with him."

She nodded and switched on the TV.

I studied her earnest face with the sad, dark eyes, wondering what she would say to Dad. I hoped that he could help her. Paula held the remote and surfed the channels, stopping at the news.

"In the local area," an anchor said, "Pikes County Tribal Police have called for an autopsy in Mindel Solomon's violent death. Classmates found the body of the young high-school student after she was reported missing from a school hunting outing. The Pikes County Tribal Police have been seeking possible witnesses."

Paula slammed off the set.

"Don't have far to look, do they?"

"What do you mean?"

"Only ones around were the archery crew and Guthrie. Besides me, that is. I'm the school photographer and I was taking pictures for the yearbook. The only weapon I had was my camera. It was Guthrie and company who had the arrows."

"Who's Guthrie?"

"Archery coach, honors English teacher, guidance counselor, football coach, collector of lost souls. He's acting principal whenever Mr. Parker's at meetings, which is practically always."

"Sounds like a dynamo. Do the kids like him?"

"Oh, yeah. Especially the ex-crackheads. He gets them off drugs by turning them onto religion."

I thought about Mr. Solomon, whose parents had sent him to an Orthodox school when he was fifteen. He had been into drugs, too. "So what's so bad about that?" I asked.

Paula shook her head. "The born-again crowd worships Mr. Guthrie like he's God himself. They follow him around like programmed robots. But if he's so godly, how come he kills animals just for sport?"

As an animal-rights person myself, I wondered about that. And another problem bothered me. "If the Solomons are Orthodox," I said, "how did Mindy manage to get out of the house to go hunting on the Sabbath?"

Paula shrugged. "Maybe she sneaks out while Daddy and Mommy are praying. It's how they spend all of their Saturdays."

"Maybe," I said not wanting to argue. I doubted it would be that easy to get out of observing the Sabbath. "So there was no one else around when it happened?" I asked. "Kids out-side of the archery club?"

"Well, I couldn't see everyone. With each holed up in their favorite spot, it was lucky I got any pictures at all. But a few party crash-ers wouldn't have surprised me in the least. It was the last hunt before vacation. A big one! They were chomping for blood. Guess some-one wanted Mindy's more than a deer's."

"She was killed with an arrow?"

"You got it."

I shivered. "But that could have been an ac-cident, couldn't it? What if she moved, and someone took her for a deer?"

"No! She was in bright orange hunting gear! Whoever shot Mindy Solomon had to have known it was a girl, not an animal. Ask any bow hunter. They'll tell you the same thing."

"I don't know any," I said, "thank God."

Paula raised her eyebrows then checked her watch. "I've got to call someone." She picked up the phone on the far wall and spoke into it as if I weren't there.

"Where are you?" I heard her say, "But why can't I come?" She listened a while. "Of course I know you didn't do it. I do trust you. But why did you run?" She listened. "What kind of danger?" She sighed. "Okay, I won't come. I promise." Paula paused again. "Yes. I'll be careful. Don't worry. I'll be okay. You just stay there and take care of yourself, you hear? I love you, too. Are you still there?" She stared at the phone. I heard her whisper, "What about your medicine?" Then she walked back toward me and switched on the TV again. We watched two dumb sitcoms and were halfway through a third when Dad and Shirley finally came home.

"Meet me tomorrow morning at nine in the photo lab," Paula said, dumping her props into her backpack. She lifted her bike into her grandmother's old station wagon, and they took off.

"How did it go, Dad?" I asked. My father closed his eyes and shook his head.

"The mother is still in shock. Moshé is in a frenzy about the funeral. Begged me to speak to the officers who were there."

"Did it help?"

My father shrugged. "I explained our law. The police explained theirs. Bottom line is that this was a violent death, and we've got to wait for an autopsy." Dad looked at the fridge.

"Guess we should have some of that food Shirley left us," I said.

We went through the motions, but neither of us ate much. Soon after dinner, Dad announced that he had work to do. As he limped toward his room, I couldn't help but ask, "Do you think Mindy could have been murdered, Dad?"

He turned at the door to the study. "It looks like Ha Shem (God) has decided we should be here a while," he said. "I figure he thinks I have work to do. But investigating this poor girl's violent death is police work, not mine. What I have to do is set this town up with a new Hebrew school."

monday

chapter 6

Pike's Landing Central could have doubled for my learning plant back home. It was just as modern and almost as ugly. I saw two sprawling, flat buildings—one the middle school, the other the high school—with a passageway between them. The stadium was surrounded by the track, which left little space for the parking lot. Finding a spot wasn't easy. Since the student section had wall-to-wall cars, I pulled up in front of a sign that read "visitors" and walked across the track.

"Excuse me!" I shouted to a sweaty runner jogging around the bend. "Which building is the high school?"

Without slowing down, he pointed to a back door where a giant Christmas wreath exploded into the gray December morning. A sign below the wreath said, "Visitors must report to the office." I ignored it and headed for the basement, where every school I know sticks the arts rooms. On my way to the stairs, kids' voices rose and fell in those crazy highs and lows that rumble through schools like a train crashing toward winter holidays. Never mind state laws against religious symbols in government places—gaudy murals garnished the walls with mangers, menorahs, and Iroquois ceremonial masks. I saw skating and sledding, people competing at snow snake and lacrosse, and the burning of the sacred tobacco. The Christmas tree wore tinsel and stars (original art class creations). The tree stretched up to the skylight on the ceiling.

Down in the basement, nothing glittered. I walked on past the pay phones, past the woodworking shop, to the door marked "photo lab."

Paula was waiting outside. "Where were you?"

I shrugged. "Finding a parking space."

"Oh, yeah, I forgot. You're one of those polluters!" She scowled. "Okay, move it or we'll miss homeroom."

I followed Paula Ash to classes, jotting down things in my notebook for my report. "The school district is very poor," I wrote, after seeing the math room computers. They were so old they could have been in the Smithsonian. The kids mostly wore jeans and were noisy in the halls, no different from my school.

In honors English, Mr. Guthrie lectured on Shakespeare's *Romeo and Juliet* then asked if anyone had questions. No one did. I studied him. With his slim physique and his crew cut, he looked almost boyish. Paula doodled a picture of him aiming an arrow at a deer and passed it to me when he wasn't looking.

In French I sympathized with the kids struggling with their accents. I remembered the hard time I had my first summer in France with my mom. I've spent so many summers there since my parents divorced that by now I can speak like everyone else around. For forty-five minutes, I fought the temptation to raise my hand and show off. I felt relieved when the bell rang and I could follow Paula to lunch.

"There's room at that table," I said, walking toward one where a couple of dark-haired kids sat. A backpack with a three sisters patch hung over a bench.

"Indian territory!" Paula said. "They don't want us any more than the rest want them."

"Prejudice?" I wrote down in the notebook in my head for later transfer to my report. Paula dragged me to a table halfway down the left side of the cafeteria.

A boy looked up from his food. "Who's that?" he asked.

"Name's Vivi. Vivi Hartman," Paula answered. "Her father is the rabbi my grandma dragged down." She held out her hands like my presence wasn't her fault.

"Aaron Kaplan," the boy said, peering at me through big horn-rimmed glasses. He pointed to the girl next to him, blue-eyed with short, blonde hair. "This is Debbie Levine."

"Josh Levy," said a broad-shouldered boy.

"You're lucky," the kid named Aaron said. "Monday is hot dogs and beans."

I smiled. "Thanks, but I brought my lunch."

Aaron shrugged. "On a scale of one to ten, hot dogs and beans are nine on the list of slop." He turned back to his book.

Paula scowled at him. "For goodness sake, Aaron, you a retard or something? I told you, her father's a rabbi. She can only eat kosher stuff." She sat and pulled me down beside her on the bench.

Debbie Levine looked at me. "Me too. It's a pain sometimes, isn't it? Only Mindy never seemed to mind it."

"I thought you loved all that primitive stuff," Aaron said to Debbie.

"Anyway, Debbie," Paula said. "We said we wouldn't talk about Mindy."

"You said that, Paula. I didn't!" Debbie retorted. Her face flushed a deep red. "The truth is, you couldn't stand her, could you?"

Aaron curled his lips in a sarcastic smile and said, "Paula couldn't have been too happy when her Indian gave her up for Mindy." He closed his book.

"You're pitiful, Aaron." Paula shook her head. "Jimmy Cloud wasn't interested in Mindy."

"Lay off, Aaron," Josh Levy said. "You know it was just Jimmy's job to teach Mindy bow holds at archery practice. Bill Hansen taught her, too. Guthrie had them both instructing beginners."

"Bill Hansen the quarterback? I wouldn't mind beginning something with him," Debbie said, smiling.

"I doubt if he scored any goals with her," Aaron said. "He just helped her with archery and brought her to Bible meetings."

"Yeah, I bet that's all he did," Paula said.

Aaron shrugged. "It wasn't Bill's idea. Mr. Guthrie was the one who thought it would be great to have someone with Mindy's background teaching Old Testament stuff. She did a good job, too."

Paula scowled. "And went from Orthodox Jew to Jesus Freak in the process. At least you didn't have that far to go. You never set foot in temple since your Bar Mitzvah."

"And you have?" Arron pointed to the three sisters patch on Paula's backpack. "To each his own."

"You don't get it at all, Aaron Kaplan, do you? I didn't become a Seneca. That patch just shows my support for their position. But you're trying to be something you're not, and in the process you've become a real Neanderthal."

"Like Jimmy Cloud?"

"Jimmy is a Seneca. Hunting is part of his culture. A sign of manhood. And unlike you guys, the Seneca don't kill animals just for sport but for sustenance."

"Yeah, well, if we're so Neolithic, what were you doing on our hunting trip?"

"My assignment! Shooting pictures of you imbeciles for the yearbook."

"Yeah? Well, I hope you caught your boyfriend in the act." Aaron grinned. "Where is your hunter today, anyway?"

"What's it to you?" Paula snapped.

"Skipping school just might lose him that NYU scholarship. Of course he probably won't be able to go, anyway. Oh well, they teach college courses in jails now, I hear. Maybe he'll get his degree from Attica."

"I thought we were talking about Mindy," Debbie said.

"We are," Aaron said. "It was way out on the

other side of Tonawanda Creek where we found her. Only archer who hunts all the way out in those woods is Jimmy Cloud."

chapter 7

Driving back to the temple, I was thinking
so hard of the lunchroom talk that I managed
to get lost. I stopped in a supermarket parking
lot and studied my map. The streets pretty
much ran east and west, and the highways
went north and south. A section of land was
outlined in red and labeled "lieu land." The
state had moved a good many Seneca to the
lieu land about thirty years ago, when the
government flooded part of the reservation to
build a utility dam.

It was almost five and already growing dark
when I finally made it back. The phone was
ringing.

"Vivi, you saw the pot roast I left to defrost
in the icebox?" Shirley asked. "All you have to

do is heat it up for dinner." I tried hard not to giggle. My grandma calls a fridge an icebox, too.

"Thanks a lot, Mrs. Imber," I said.

"My pleasure. You'll call Paula to the phone, like a good girl, yes?"

"Paula? Isn't she home? She left on her bike right after school."

Shirley's voice rose. "She's not there?"

"Nuh-uh, Mrs. Imber. Maybe she went to a friend's house," I said.

"A friend?"

"Yes. Maybe Debbie?"

"No, Vivi. Debbie is working in her father's dollar store. He's very busy before the holidays. I just came from there."

I hesitated. "Well, Paula has other friends, doesn't she?"

The silence at the other end was scary. When Shirley finally spoke, her voice shook.

"Vivi, you'll get your father right away. Bring him to my daughter's house. Number Seven, on Old Post Road." A set of directions followed so fast I could barely write them all down.

Once on the road, I knew I'd driven out this way before, but I still felt unsure of my route. When I came to Harry Blacksnake's gas station, I pulled to the edge of the road and checked my map. Old Post Road was less than a quarter of a mile beyond.

"Guess she lives on the lieu land," I said.

Dad wrinkled his forehead. "I thought only Indians lived there."

Number Seven was a square yellow shack. The wind had picked up, rustling frosty tinted stalks in the desolate looking backyard vegetable garden. Compared to its closest neighbor—an ancient trailer on blocks—Number Seven was a palace. A snarling German shepherd, straining against a chain anchored into the hard ground, stood guard over Shirley's old station wagon. He had to outweigh Farfel by sixty pounds. My father murmured a prayer and moved his crutches toward the house. I slinked out of the beast's reach to join Dad and help him up the cracked steps. The Israeli olive wood mezuzah, with a plate of embossed brass, looked way out of synch. Dad didn't seem to notice. Whatever the appearance of the outer case, inside was a tightly rolled parchment with the first two verses of the prayer "Hear O Israel." Dad touched it, kissed his fingers, and looked at me. I observed the ritual then banged the rusty knocker. Shirley Imber opened the door a crack, peered at us through red-rimmed eyes, then opened it wider.

"Enough already, Rembrandt! Thank you for coming, Rabbi. Here, Vivi, give me your coats.

There are hooks in the kitchen." She took our coats and came back with a basket. "Please sit. Have an apple. You'll forgive me for not offering you anything else, Rabbi. But it's not kosher here. My daughter gave up religion a long time ago. You saw the mezuzah? Lee laughed at me when I put it up there. 'You think a little box with the "Hear O Israel" prayer is going to keep trouble away from my house?' she asked me. I try my best to teach my grand-child, but . . . ," Shirley shrugged.

Dad nodded. I plopped down on the old green couch and picked out the largest apple in the basket. The living room was an eight-by-ten rectangle, the walls covered with prints of pictures by Chagall, Picasso, Miro, and other artists my grandma had taught me about. Among them hung two glossy, framed photos. One was a wide-angle view of the utility dam and reservoir. The other showed a woman at work at an easel, her auburn hair caught up in a green ribbon, her brush poised over a half-finished picture of a child with almond-shaped eyes. Shirley followed my gaze.

"That's my daughter, Lee," she said. "Paula took those pictures and framed them herself." Her lips trembled. "She always comes here right after school to feed and walk the dog. What could have happened to her?"

The only response came from outside the

house where Rembrandt yipped and yelped. Above the canine racket, I heard the squeal of a bike stopping short. Then Paula walked through the doorway, a camera swinging across her chest. Her jacket was muddy, her jeans torn at the knees. There was a scrape on her cheek and one above her left eyebrow. I stared at her, and Shirley grabbed her in a bear hug. "Thank God! You're safe! But what happened to you?"

"Nothing." Paula tossed her red braid and collapsed onto the couch.

"Nothing?" her grandmother shouted. "Look at you!"

Paula sighed. "No big deal. My tire got caught in a pothole is all. I got thrown. Landed in that ditch over by Blacksnake's filling station. Harry pulled me out." She bit her lip, then glanced at me warily. I could tell she was lying, but her grandmother didn't seem to notice.

"That bike! It will be the death of you!" Shirley said. "Why can't you ride the bus like the other kids?"

"That pollution missile? No thanks."

Shirley turned to Dad. "I give up. Maybe you can talk some sense into her, Rabbi."

As she blurted out a list of anti-Paula complaints, I pointed to the utility dam photo. "You did a great job on that one," I told her.

Paula grimaced. "Yeah. I keep it there to re-mind me how bad the state stinks. You know how many families were kicked out of their houses because of that monstrosity?"

I shrugged. "But the Seneca still own part of the land out there, don't they?"

Her eyes flashed. "Sure. Only thing is, it's clear under the dam. It's like, 'Come into my parlor. Sorry if it's damp.'" She groaned as she stood up, then made her way into the kitchen. A few minutes later, she came limping back, carrying a fleece jacket and a leash. "I've got to go walk the dog," she said, dragging one foot.

I shook my head. "I can do that. You should take care of those cuts or they'll get infected."

"Thanks," Paula said.

Out in the yard, Rembrandt barked. I shiv-ered. You and your big mouth, Vivi Hartman, I chided myself. You must have been crazy to offer to walk that beast. My father turned to me. "So what are you waiting for, Vivi? It isn't every day one gets a chance to do a mitzvah."

For the chance to do this kind of good deed, I could have waited forever. But Paula was helping me on with her warm coat. Grasping my apple in one hand, I held out the other for the leash.

Out on the cracked step, I turned to see Paula watching me through the window. I looked up at the cloudy sky and whispered,

"You know how much I love animals. But this one.... If only you'll help, I'll give half my allowance to the SPCA next month." Then, reaching into my pocket, I walked up to the snarling Rembrandt and handed him the apple. As he worked on it, I clipped on his leash. "Heel!" I yelled and looked straight ahead as I walked out of the yard. To my absolute amazement, the shepherd matched every step.

With only a few dim lights from the trailers scattered across the landscape, it was hard to see the dirt road. But Rembrandt seemed to know where he was going, stopping at some trees, passing others by as if they weren't worth the effort. When he finally squatted and pooped, I turned back toward the house, but Rembrandt wasn't quite ready to go home. He pulled me toward a light about a half-mile down the road, right into Harry Blacksnake's filling station. The closer he got, the more Rembrandt yipped. As Harry came out of his store, Rembrandt tore from my grasp and ran to him.

"So fella, ready for your treat, are you?" Harry scratched Rembrandt's ear and stuck a giant milkbone in the dog's mouth. "Your girl too beat up to walk you tonight, is she?"

"She is pretty beat up, Mr. Blacksnake," I said. The man peered at me. I walked beneath the lamppost. Harry Blacksnake nodded.

"Oh, the rabbi's kid. You a friend of Paula's?"

"Sort of. She said you pulled her out of a ditch right near here?"

"Why? You aiming to jump in, too?"

"Jump? What do you mean? She said she got stuck in a pothole and was thrown."

"Pothole? So that's what she said, was it? There was no pothole, girlie. He came right at her and forced her into that ditch."

"Who?"

"The kid who was tailing her in the truck."

"But why would anyone do that to Paula?"

Harry scowled. "I'm not a psychic, lady. I just fill cars. All I know is how she got in the ditch. Landed hard, she did. Lucky that camera around her neck didn't choke her."

I stared at him. The camera! That was it! Paula was the school photographer. She'd taken pictures of the hunt. That must be what the truck driver wanted. I looked at Harry.

"How do you know it was a kid in the truck?"

Harry shrugged. "Old wreck was so covered with primer, it looked like an orange. That vehicle was in the middle of a paint job. Only a kid would be so antsy to drive, he couldn't wait until it was done."

"Did you get the license?" I asked.

Harry laughed. "Wouldn't do much good,

would it? He had to have stole it."

"The truck?"

"You crazy, girl? Not even a kid would steal an old heap like that. But the plate, that was different. Stuck in the window like he'd just snatched it! Nothing and no one's safe around here anymore. Go on home, girl. It's late. I've got to get me some supper." My stomach moaned at his words.

"You have candy bars in your store?" I asked.

"If you got the cash, I got the merchandise."

I felt in my pockets for some change, but all that was there was Dad's credit card. And Harry Blacksnake didn't take credit cards.

"On second thought, I'd better not spoil my appetite," I said.

"Okay." Harry waved and walked toward his store.

Rembrandt wagged his tail.

"Sure," I said, picking up the leash, "you had a milkbone and an apple." The lights in Harry's station went out and the road ahead was black as pitch. I thought about poor Paula lying in the ditch and shivered. Thank God she came out of that ditch okay!

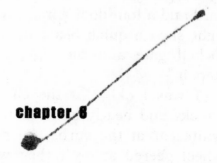

chapter 8

Seneca fires cast a glow in the night sky as Dad and I headed back to the temple. At least, I thought that's where we were headed. I was wrong.

"Take the next left to Lafayette Street," my father said. "I need to stop in at the Solomon house."

"Stop? Dad, I'm starving!"

"So am I. But the older Solomon boys got home from Israel today. I want to offer them my condolences. It's not far—the brick house on the northwest corner of Lafayette and Elm."

Strictly speaking, the Solomon house wasn't on the corner. It was at least twenty yards away. The corner was a hole of gaping rock with a yellow forklift and dump truck at its edge. It was separated from the rest of the lot by a high cyclone fence, which circled a paved yard and a four-door garage. A rotating searchlight shed a quick beam of light on the padlocked gate and the sign, "Solomon's Auto Repair."

I was looking at the enclosure's resident wrecks and nearly bumped into the blue and white car at the curb. The policeman at the wheel peered at my father, who rolled down his window.

"Hi, Rabbi," the officer said. The short, dark hair below his cap framed the high cheekbones and flat nose common to the Iroquois. He squinted his almond-shaped eyes and looked past Dad, at me.

"Good evening, Lieutenant Jemison. This is my daughter, Aviva," Dad answered. "Why the searchlight?"

The policeman touched his cap. "There was some trouble here last night."

"What kind of trouble?"

He pointed to a boarded-up window in the garage. "Someone threw a brick through that window. The brick had a note wrapped around it. Read 'Go back to Brooklyn, daughter killer!'"

"Anyone hurt?" Dad asked.

"No, just property damage. Could have been worse. Could have set off that load of dynamite Solomon's been using to blast that hole for his used car lot."

"Any idea who did it?"

Jemison shrugged. "Yes. We got him. Sóme nut with a grudge and a few too many drinks inside him. Said Solomon sold him a bad used car and should be run out of town." He grimaced. "Not that we didn't expect this kind of thing."

"What do you mean?"

"Someone commits a crime and folks get out the war glue. Attach all the old hatreds that aren't connected."

Daughter killer! I shivered and thought about the newscast I'd heard and tried to recall everything Paula and the other kids had told me about Mindy Solomon's death. Why would anyone suspect her father, an Orthodox man? He certainly wasn't a hunter. Or was he? I recalled the young Moshé who Shirley had described—the drinker, the druggie, the truant— whose desperate parents had sent him away. But not until he was fifteen years old. What if, back in those days, Moshé Solomon had learned to be pretty good with the bow? What if it wasn't a kid who had sideswiped Paula? What better place than an auto repair shop to stash a truck with the primer still on it? No Jewish man as Orthodox as Moshé Solomon would ever leave his house during

Shivah. But the police still had not released Mindy's body, and Shivah could not begin until after the funeral.

I watched Lieutenant Jemison get into his car. "Well, have a good one, Rabbi," he said. "Goodnight, miss." He spun the blue-and-white around. I waved to him then pulled ahead and stopped in front of the house.

Dad and I followed custom and didn't knock, just kissed the mezuzah and stepped inside to the hall, where a white sheet draped the mirror. The covered mirror was a sign of mourning. The big, orange ball wasn't. It bounced down the stairs and landed at my feet as four kids, two girls and two boys, looked down at me from the top.

"Enough already! You'll wake up the baby," a dark-bearded man commanded over his shoulder. He wore a black skullcap, black pants, and a flowing black coat. He glanced at me.

"My daughter, Aviva," Dad said.

Moshé Solomon turned to the stairs. "Hendel, Rifka, come down. Take the *maidel* to your room. Show her your schoolwork." I sat on the floor with the girls checking first-grade math problems and spelling words, then listened as they read from an old-fashioned primer, which went well with their ankle-length, long-sleeved dresses and laced-up leather shoes. Every so often, they stopped and, smiling shyly, touched my hair or my jeans. If their older brothers had come home from Israel like Dad said, the girls never mentioned them, and I never got to see them.

A half-hour later, we were on our way back to the temple. The car was freezing, and the steering wheel felt like ice. I stuck a hand in my pocket, hoping for gloves. But what I pulled out was no glove. It wasn't even a mitten.

It was a small canister of film.

tuesday

chapter 9

"Why, after all these years, do we still read Shakespeare?" Mr. Guthrie looked around the room.

A guy in a football jersey yawned. "'Cause we got to pass a test on it."

Kids laughed. Mr. Guthrie smiled. Across the aisle, Paula doodled a picture of corn, beans, and squash in her notebook.

"Why did you give it to me?" I whispered.

"Give you what?"

"You know what. The film you put in my pocket last night."

Mr. Guthrie glared at me. "Ms. Hartman, perhaps you can tell us why Shakespeare is still popular."

Everyone turned to stare at me. I sank down

into my seat, my voice barely audible. "Because his plays can still make people mad?"

"Explain that, please," the teacher said. He might almost look like a student, but the authority in his voice said, "I gotcha!"

I took a breath. "Well, take *Hamlet*, for instance. Hamlet says in the second scene, 'Frailty, thy name is woman.' My best friend, Rachael, goes bonkers at that line. You have to admit, Shakespeare does make girls sound like birdbrains sometimes."

Titters.

"And look at the way Shakespeare shows Moors in *Othello*," I said, encouraged. "But the one that raises my blood pressure the most is his anti-Semitic stereotype, Shylock, in *The Merchant of Ven—*"

"Thank you, Ms. Hartman," Mr. Guthrie said. "I think we all get the idea." He turned to the blackboard. In large block letters, he wrote "politically charged."

"So why did you give it to me?" I asked Paula again after class, as we walked down the crowded, noisy corridor.

"Because no one would figure you have it. It's the film I shot of the hunt. Someone wants it bad. Just hold on to it until I can develop it, okay?"

I bit my lip. "I don't know, Paula. Maybe you should give it to the police. It might be evidence. It's wrong—"

Paula glared at me. "Yeah, right and wrong, that's your father's thing, isn't it? What would you guys do without it?"

"Starve!" I grinned. "And eating's my favorite sport."

"Very funny!" Paula paused. "But you can forget about me giving it to the police."

"Okay, Paula, but level with me. Are you afraid there's a photo that casts suspicion on Jimmy?"

Paula's shoulders sagged. "Just as I got my camera set up to take the team picture, I saw him walking away toward his special place. His grandfather used to take him there when he was little, he told me. He told me he likes it there, far from the rest, where he doesn't have to dress up in orange like a clown."

"Where is this place?"

"Up near Tonawanda Creek. And now they found her body out there." Paula's eyes moistened. "He looked so great that morning, I just had to get a shot of him. Don't you see what Bill Hansen and his Militia of God will do if they get hold of it? Ever since Jimmy won that college scholarship, they've been waiting to pick his bones clean. As if that will help solve the land lease problem! Me and my pictures! It's not only the militia. How will it look to everyone?"

"It looks worse that he ran away, I think. Can't you convince him to come back?"

Paula shook her head.

"Do you know where he is?"

"Yes."

"Where you called him at?"

"No, it's a cell phone."

"Who else knows?"

"People he can trust."

"Okay," I said. "But we can't hold on to the film much longer, Paula—it's too dangerous. I'll keep the film until this afternoon. Then I'll bring it to your house and help you develop the pictures, okay?"

Paula shook her head. "I don't have a darkroom at home. And I can only use the school lab during lunch and after classes."

I stared at her. "Does everybody know that?"

"So what if they do?"

"Were you in the darkroom yesterday?"

"No. Why are you questioning me?"

"I'm using pilpul."

"My grandmother told me about that. It's that old Torah logic, right?"

"Right. Our sages used it to figure out what each passage means. The rules are very involved, but my own simple form might go something like this: One, if you weren't in the darkroom yesterday, anyone following you would know that you hadn't developed the film yet. Two, if you hadn't developed it, he might guess that you had it with you. Three, if whoever killed Mindy thought you had a picture of him doing it, he sure would want to grab it before you could show it around. Don't you see, Paula? This might have nothing to do with nailing Jimmy."

Paula nodded. "It sounds logical, I guess."

"So whose picture did you shoot that morning?"

"You must be kidding. I didn't take notes. At one time or another, I must have got all of them. Except for poor Mindy." Paula's lip trembled. "Sorry, Vivi, I can't talk anymore now. Just hold the film for a little longer, okay? Meet me in the photo lab at the beginning of lunch."

"Okay," I answered.

Paula started forward then stopped. "Be careful with the film, Vivi. Don't let anyone know you have it. Promise me."

"I promise," I said.

chapter 10

My stomach growled as I hurried across the dim, chilly basement, already tasting my sandwich although it was still in its brown paper sack. Salami on rye. I had brought two of them and decided to give one to Paula, never dreaming she'd chicken out. But there was the sign, "photo lab closed!" I knocked anyway. No answer.

"Paula?" I called.

Nothing.

I tried the knob. It stuck at first, then gave. The room had high, narrow windows. I stared at the jumble of photos and film lying everywhere. A large wooden desk was standing on end.

"Paula!" I called again, tearing at a black

curtain that hung from ceiling to floor. I ripped it aside and walked into the small, dark cubicle. I wrinkled up my nose at the odor. Fixative! The prints on the floor looked glossy and wet. In the double sink, other prints were soaking.

"Paula?" I said weakly, knowing there wouldn't be an answer. A shiver went through me as I headed out of the darkroom, out of the photo lab, and into the hall.

"Ms. Hartman?" Mr. Guthrie smiled. "What are you doing down here? Lose your way?"

"P-P-Paula," I stammered.

The teacher nodded toward the lab.

I shook my head. "Not there."

Mr. Guthrie walked past me into the room. "Good Lord!" He turned and bolted for the steps, his long legs taking two, three at a time. I sprinted up after him.

The clerk in the office stared at us. "Mr. Guthrie? What's wrong?"

But the teacher didn't answer. He pushed past her to a console and picked up a microphone. "Paula Ash. Report to the office, please. Paula Ash. Report to the office at once!"

"I guess she's not here, Mr. Guthrie," the clerk said after a while. "I guess she cut out, like the kids sometimes do. I'll report it to Mr. Parker when he comes back from his meeting with the Board."

"But she wouldn't just cut out," I shouted. "She was supposed to meet me at twelve."

Mr. Guthrie dropped the mike and looked at me hard. Right then, he didn't appear boyish. "Anything you want to tell me, Ms. Hartman?"

I opened my mouth to tell him about the film, then remembered my promise to Paula and opened my backpack instead. The marvelous smell invaded the office.

"Salami," I said. "I was bringing her a kosher salami sandwich."

Mr. Guthrie moved his lips like he was counting. "Anything else?"

I closed my eyes and looked upward. He did say 'want to tell him,' didn't he?

"No sir," I said. "Don't you think we should call the police?"

Mr. Guthrie sighed. "We don't call the police for student pranks. I'll soon know what this is all about. And when I do catch the rascal, he'll sit in detention until Doomsday, Ms. Hartman," he said. We're not like your cold, big-city schools. Most of our students are God-fearing kids like my own. Our school is like a family. We have to preserve its integrity. Better to air the laundry at home."

Maybe so. But as soon as I got out of there, I took my laundry list to the phone in the girls' lavatory and dropped in my quarter. The only family I had in Pikes Landing didn't answer.

My extended family, Shirley, didn't answer either. With that spry old woman as chauffeur, Dad could be at the Solomons', the funeral home . . . anywhere. After twenty rings, I hung up the phone.

chapter 11

"Coffee?" the lieutenant asked. He looked tired and grim and was holding a blue cup.

"No, thanks."

"Pop?"

"A Pepsi would be good."

The lieutenant went to a small fridge. I looked up at a giant wall calendar with a picture of a bunch of men ice fishing on a lake. The men were holding cans of beer. The caption said, "Winter or summer, the best catch is a Miller." I wondered if the policeman would rather be out fishing on a frozen lake with his buddies than here in his steamy office, talking to a girl who didn't like coffee, just pop.

He handed me a can of Coke. Then he sat down and leaned back in his chair. "So Mr.

Guthrie thought that the photo lab business was just a student prank, Aviva?"

"I guess. I mean, that's what he called it."

"Then he wasn't all that upset about it?"

"Well, I wouldn't say that."

"Why wouldn't you say that, Aviva?"

"Well, when he first saw the mess, he turned pale and practically flew up the stairs to the office."

"That's when he made the announcement?"

"Yes. But Paula was a no-show, so he gave up."

"I see." The lieutenant leaned forward. "And after that, he told you how God-fearing the kids are and gave you the 'school's a family' sermon?"

"Yes."

"What happened next?"

"I tried to call Mrs. Imber and my dad, but neither of them was home. So I called you, and you said to come down."

The lieutenant nodded. "Is there anything else you want to tell me?"

That "want" word again! I shook my head.

The lieutenant pushed away from his desk. "Well, Aviva, thank you for stopping by. There's not much the police can do, far as I can tell."

I jumped up. "Nothing? But you're the police! What about Paula? What about the room? What else has to happen before you can do something?"

Lieutenant Jemison folded his arms across his chest and looked at me. "The rest of the story might do it."

Outside the window, a policeman fought the wind to get to a blue-and-white. The library's arrow-shaped sign whipped back and forth on its chains. I forced my eyes back to the policeman's desk. On one side of it were a phone and a tape recorder. On the other side were some papers under a clay paperweight, which had a picture of corn, beans, and squash. I thought about the emblem on the Indian kids' backpacks—on Paula's backpack.

"She'll never trust me again," I said. But even as I said it, I knew how dumb it was. Unless I told Lieutenant Jemison everything, Paula might not live to trust anyone. I dug the film out of my backpack and laid it on the officer's desk. "Paula asked me to hold this," I said. "Someone's been very anxious to get it from her."

The lieutenant turned on the tape recorder. "Go on," he said, and I told him about Paula's telephone conversation with Jimmy and about the pickup truck forcing Paula into the ditch.

My father looked at my untouched food. He cut off a chunk of bread. "I know how you feel. Doing the right thing is usually harder than doing the wrong thing."

I waited, knowing the words were just openers.

He picked up his butter knife and spread the butter slowly, evenly. "But what's even harder is figuring out what the right thing is," Dad said and looked at me. "You figured right, ya-keerati. The police have an all points bulletin out. With God's help, they'll find Paula soon and—"

Farfel's bark cut him off. Even before the bell rang, my small dog was jumping at the door. Dad looked through the glass.

"Rabbi? It's me, Jemison." Dad opened the door and let him in. The policeman's face had even more tired lines than before.

I studied him warily. "Please sit down," Dad said, and he poured the policeman a cup of coffee. "Have you found Paula yet?"

The policeman shook his head. "I need some help, Rabbi. Last one to see her was a girl named Debbie Levine who was with her in science class." He took a handkerchief from his pocket and mopped his forehead. "It seems Paula told Debbie she had an appointment this afternoon at four o'clock." He looked at Dad hard. "And that appointment was with you."

I stared at the policeman. Paula hadn't wasted any time calling my father for an appointment. Dad nodded.

"Unfortunately, she never made it."

"Could you tell me why you had planned to

meet with her?" Jemison asked.

"I can assure you," Dad said. "It was a strictly personal and somewhat religious matter."

"I see." For a moment I thought the policeman would be satisfied with that, but he seemed to change his mind.

"Are you sworn to secrecy then?"

"Not in a religious sense, but it is a private matter and has nothing to do with Mindy Solomon."

The lieutenant nodded. "Let me be the judge of that."

Dad sighed. "Paula wanted to speak to me about her mother. Lee Ash is an *aguna,* a chained woman. Although she and her husband divorced in the civil court nine years ago, the Orthodox husband won't grant her a religious divorce. Without the religious divorce, she cannot marry again in any but a reform ceremony. The whole sordid business made Lee Ash turn away from religion, and Paula and her grandmother are worried. The first day I got here, the child asked if she could see me very soon. It seems she had read the book I wrote on how some of us rabbis are working to free these women, and she wants me to try to help her mother." He looked at the policeman. "Have you any other leads?" Dad asked, as if the previous subject was closed.

Jemison seemed to consider. "Maybe," he answered. "We think she's with a friend, Jimmy Cloud, who has been missing since Saturday— since the school hunting outing, in fact. He lives over in the lieu near the Ash family. Jimmy's mother is concerned, too. She's a widow. He's her only child."

"I should think she'd be frantic," Dad said.

"She wasn't at first. Said he's into the old religion. He often goes off to meditate by himself."

"Then what is she worried about?"

"His health. He's a diabetic and needs his insulin, and she isn't sure he took it with him. He's never been away for this long without medication."

The lieutenant turned to me. "Paula ever mention running away to join Jimmy Cloud?"

"Not to me," I said. "But if she were with Jimmy, I don't think he'd hurt her."

"Oh?" The policeman raised his eyebrows. "Why is that?"

"I told you before, I heard her on the phone. They love each other. She trusts him."

"I see. Well, thank you, Aviva." The policeman nodded. Then he asked Dad, "Would an Orthodox man be upset if his daughter dated a boy of another religion?"

"Absolutely." Dad grimaced. "Dating can lead to marriage. To marry a non-Jewish man would be considered worse than death. If a daughter married out of the religion, her father would sit through the seven days of mourning, just as Moshé Solomon must do now."

"Thank you, Rabbi." The policeman stood up. "You can do your funeral tomorrow."

"Then you have the autopsy report?"

"Oh, yes. Mindel Solomon died at seven a.m. She was strangled with her own scarf, which was then placed neatly over her face."

I stared at him. "But what about the arrow?"

Jemison shrugged. "All we know for sure is that the arrow wasn't what killed her." He stood up, thanked us, and left.

Strangled? Oh, that poor girl! My eyes blurred as my mind went into pilpul mode. One, if Mindy had died of strangulation, the killer wouldn't have to be such a hotshot archer, hitting her right in the heart. And two, unless, of course, he was trying to make it appear that the arrow did the job.

"It's getting late, Vivi," Dad said. "Don't you have some report work to do? We have to be up early for the funeral."

"But I don't think I'll go to the school tomorrow, Dad, unless Paula turns up there for me to follow around."

My father shook his head. "But you still have to do your report. You'll go after the funeral."

He went to his study. A few minutes later, I

heard him on the phone calling temple members about the funeral. "Afterwards there will be a meeting," he said, "to discuss the new Hebrew school. We owe it to our children."

wednesday

chapter 12

The sky was dark. A blanket of gray fog enveloped us, breached here and there by a bright woolen winter coat. People shuffled and molded their boots into the remnants of early morning snow. Around dawn, the snow had stopped falling and left the wind with only dry leaves to blow about.

I shivered as I watched Mindy Solomon's older brothers, Dov and Noah. They lifted the plain pine box from the hearse. According to custom, they had ripped the lapels of their black coats in mourning. In the flapping coats and their broad-brimmed black hats, they looked like two giant ravens as they carried their sister's coffin to the burial plot. The taller boy shouted orders at the temple members who would lower the coffin into the earth. One of the members was Josh Levy.

A few feet away, I saw Shirley, her eyes red and dry, staring at the grave.

"Paula!" she cried suddenly, flinging herself toward the coffin.

"It's not Paula, Mama. It's Mindy," a woman said gently. "Paula will be okay. You'll see." The woman wore a green wool cap over her long, red hair. Her cheeks glowed red with cold. She was beautiful.

"You hear about Paula? She's missing," Debbie Levine whispered, coming up to me. "And the morning paper said Mindy was strangled. How horrible!"

I nodded, still looking at Paula's mom, wondering who had called her about Paula. Shirley or Lieutenant Jemison? I wondered if the lieutenant was here at the funeral. Then I saw him standing quietly at the edge of the crowd. His eyes moved to a face, paused and focused on another, then came to rest on a group of students standing with Mr. Guthrie.

Debbie was looking at them, too. Her nostrils flared. "They'll probably give a twenty-one arrow salute." But the kids around Mr. Guthrie weren't holding bows. They were holding prayer books. As the teacher moved his lips, they moved theirs, too.

"The Lord is my shepherd," they sang.

Debbie was watching Aaron raise his voice along with them.

"Sing it in Hebrew, I dare you, you fink," she whispered. She turned toward the line of people waiting to throw dirt onto the coffin. As a man put down the shovel, she picked it up and took her turn. I looked at Aaron and saw his eyes cast down, as if he was ashamed that he wasn't with us. I wasn't angry like Debbie. I just felt sad that Aaron needed to be someone other than himself.

By ten o'clock, it was over. "He remembereth that we are dust," my father said. As they left the grounds, the family members repeated the words. They plucked some grass and threw it behind their backs. Then, raising earthen pitchers, they poured water over each other's hands.

The mourners drifted toward their cars. "I'll ride back to the temple with Shirley and her daughter," my father said. "I'm expecting a lot of parents at the meeting about the Hebrew school."

"Hey, Vivi," Debbie called, "My car's in the repair shop. Give me a lift back to school?"

"Sure," I said, opening the door. "Jump in." But getting away from the cemetery wasn't easy. As we approached the main gate, traffic slowed, then stopped completely. Kids with banners were clogging up the exit to the road. They were the same ones who had held prayer books only a few minutes ago.

"Justice for white women! Help find Jimmy Cloud!" they chanted.

"Between these cowboys and the Seneca with the flaming tires, we might as well give up wheels," Debbie said.

"I wonder where Mr. Guthrie is," I answered.

Debbie sniffed. "Probably took off on his trusty stallion. He's never around when there's a shootout. But not to worry, he always leaves his loyal lieutenant, Bill Hansen. He's the one who led the search team to Mindy's body after she had been missing a long time."

"That's interesting."

Debbie shrugged. "He's always the leader. Three weeks ago he led the way when his gang dropped a grenade in a Seneca doctor's clinic."

"Why did they do that?"

"They say she's a witch doctor who casts spells on little white babies. And they spread a rumor that she does abortions. The whole thing is crazy. She has a degree in endocrinology. Specializes in diabetes because there's so much of it around here. Jimmy Cloud was livid. She's his aunt. Haven't you heard the latest rumor?"

"What rumor?"

"They're saying that Jimmy got a lot of girls in trouble and took them there. They're saying maybe he got Mindy in trouble and took her there too. What a joke! Luckily, the grenade landed in the yard—and it didn't even go off."

"Did the jerks get caught?"

"Sure. The police hauled them in and the judge made their parents pay a big fine."

"What about the kids?"

"They wound up with five weeks of community service. Mostly picking up dog poop in the parks."

I studied the kids, looking for violent types, but they all seemed so ordinary—your typical boys next door.

"That's Bill Hansen," Debbie said. She pointed to a hatless, blond boy who was gesturing frantically to the group. I recognized him as the smart aleck from English class, who had answered the teacher's question so sarcastically. Sirens screamed, and I saw three blue-and-whites leave the road and screech to a stop.

"On your face!" a policeman yelled. Aaron hit the ground with the others. But not before our eyes met. He had the kind of smile that says you're scared—that if you weren't smiling, you'd be crying your eyes out.

"I hate you, Aaron Kaplan!" Debbie shrieked. "I despise you! Detest you! Abhor you! And I'm not going to the prom with any jailbird!"

"You must really like him a lot," I said.

chapter 13

Debbie didn't speak the rest of the way back to school, and I knew she was thinking about Aaron. Inside the school, the bell had rung, yet the halls were practically empty. In the cafeteria, voices echoed.

"Where is everyone?" I asked.

"It's the same every year. Tomorrow's the first day of the Seneca Midwinter Festival, up in Hiawartha Rocks. Most of the Seneca kids already took off to get ready, and a lot of other kids skip classes." The lunch table was too long for just the two of us. Too close. Too quiet.

Debbie asked, "Do you have a boyfriend?" I told her about Mike and about how he was spending his school break in Florida.

"He should be with you, not in Florida," she said. But I knew she was really thinking about Aaron and her, rather than Mike and me. "For a time, there were the three of us," she said after a while. "The only Jewish girls in our school. Now there are only Paula and me "

"Are you and Paula close friends?"

Debbie sniffed. "The only thing close to Paula is that camera around her neck."

"There's Rembrandt," I said.

"Who?"

"Her dog."

"Never met him. I never went to her house. My mom thinks her mother is weird, never going to temple, not even on holidays! And living out there on the lieu land with all those Indians, and the way she lets Paula date Jimmy Cloud." Debbie bit off a nail and rolled the broken-off piece between her fingers. "I never went to Mindy's house either, not that I would want to go there. Even Mindy wanted out." Debbie frowned. "Now that she's dead, I have these crazy thoughts, and I can't even discuss them with my parents."

"How come?"

Debbie stared at her nails. "They say it's preposterous." She selected a nail. "They keep warning me not to get involved. But what if he killed her?"

"Who?"

"Her father." Debbie started on a corner of her fingernail, worked her way around, and let a quarter moon drop into her hand. "Sounds crazy doesn't it? But there's lots you don't know."

Debbie was right. There was a lot I didn't know, and I was almost scared to find out. But not knowing was even more scary, so I asked, "Like what?"

"Like what happened two months ago, when the principal sent for Paula and me. He told us he needed a kosher home for a student. Well, that let Paula off the hook. I thought it was the same as always—a girl from some visiting orchestra or team. I figured he didn't call Mindy because her family was so strict that a kid wouldn't be allowed to do anything but pray. So I volunteered our house. I knew my parents would be cool about it. They feel it's a mitzvah to put up kosher kids from out of town. I just didn't expect her to arrive the same day."

"But she did?"

Debbie nodded. "Just before last period, the nurse sent for me. When I got to the health office, Mindy was there. She had two grocery bags full of clothes. My mother told me later that they had come from the Salvation Army. Mother said when the principal called her and told her he had an abused Jewish girl, and who it was, she could hardly believe it. He told her not to worry. They were keeping it all hush-hush. He said the school is like—"

"A family?" I asked.

"Right. How did you know?"

"I've heard it before. So Mindy went home with you?"

"Gladly."

"How long did she stay?"

"That time? About five days. Then the guidance counselor, Mr. Guthrie, told her she could go home."

"What do you mean, 'that time?'"

"There were three. All in the last two months." Debbie studied the nail on her pinky. "You know something? I don't think she wanted to go home. Who would? You should have seen those black-and-blue marks all over her arms and legs. She wore jeans and long-sleeve shirts so that no one could tell."

"She was all bruised?"

"Well, I never saw her undressed. And there were never any marks on her face."

I bit my lip. "That figures. On the face they would show. What a brute!"

"But the marks on her arms and legs would show in a short-sleeved top and a short skirt, wouldn't they?"

"Right, except you know as well as I do that Orthodox girls aren't supposed to wear those. Maybe she changed when she got to school, but

I'll bet you anything that when her parents were around, she wore high-necked dresses that came below her calves, with long sleeves, too. As for jeans, perish the thought! Only men can wear trousers. That girl must have had guts to rebel against those rules." I looked at Debbie. "What I can't understand is why her mother didn't stop him. Unless he beat her up too?"

Debbie shook her head. "I don't think so. Whenever Mrs. Solomon comes into my father's store, she seems happy and smiles a lot. The little girls are always cheerful and look so cute in their long dresses. The boys look kind of strange in those black pants and coats and their little side curls, but they're always laughing and running around and begging their mother for toys. Poor Mindy was the only one who looked sad. With the way they treated her, no wonder she was always down in the guidance office. She had to talk to someone." Debbie looked at her watch. "I'd better go and change for gym. The BOCES garage guys are mostly Seneca. I hope they didn't leave yet. I want to pick up my car after classes."

A Board of Cooperative Education Services garage. Only kids worked there. What better place to get hold of a pickup covered with primer?

"We have a BOCES garage at my school, too," I said. "Does yours do paint jobs?"

"Sure," Debbie answered.

I knew I had to get inside that garage. "What about automatic locks?" I asked her.

She shrugged. "I don't know. I guess they do everything."

"I can wait for you after school and take you home in case your car's not ready, Debbie," I offered.

"Thanks." Debbie stood up. "I'd appreciate that. The garage is in back of the stadium, all the way down at the other end of the campus, and it's so cold today."

"No problem. Be at the back door when school gets out, and I'll drive you over there."

For the rest of the day, classes were a joke. With so few kids in each room, the teachers didn't even try to teach anything. It's a good thing, too. All I could think about was Paula. When school was finally over, Debbie and I hurried out into the snow.

chapter 14

The wind howled as we drove up to the low, brick building. A hard gust whipped at the sign on top. I read, "Auto Repair Shop—Board of Cooperative Education Services."

"Anyone here?" Debbie yelled, banging on the door.

"Hold onto your reins, I'm coming," I heard. The door opened a crack. "Come on in, quick," the guy said, ushering us into the small office. "It's freezing!" He wore overalls and a heavy sweater. A gold earring with charms of the three sisters dangled from his left lobe, sticking out below his dark hair. He looked about seventeen.

"This is Vivi Hartman," Debbie told him.

The boy held out his hand.

"Rollie Hawkes." We shook.

"My wheels ready, Rollie?" Debbie asked him.

"What kind of vehicle was it?"

"My Chevy. You wrote it down. Needed a tire realignment, remember?"

"Oh, sure thing. What was the license number again?" Debbie told him and Rollie went out into the huge parking lot that surrounded the garage. While we waited, I looked through a window into the cavernous garage. A car was up on a lift, with its guts exposed. Two kids in greasy clothes were operating on it with wrenches. I turned back to look out at the parking lot and saw Rollie get into Debbie's car. He drove it up to the door and came back inside.

When Debbie had finished paying, I turned to him and asked, "I need someone to fix the automatic lock on my Dodge Caravan. Would you have time now?"

Rollie looked at his watch. "Depends. I'll have to check it out. You can sit over there." I took a seat on a hard wooden bench while he finished lecturing Debbie about checking the oil more often.

"Thanks again, Vivi," she said and started to leave. Suddenly, I was frightened. What a dumb idea. With Debbie gone, I'd be alone with these guys. What if I found that they were the ones with the orange pickup that ran Paula off the road?

"Do me a favor, Debbie?" I asked loud enough for anyone around to hear. "Call my father and tell him where I am and why. Tell him if I'm not back by four-thirty, he should send someone to get me."

"Sure," Debbie said. Rollie held out his hand for my key, then walked Debbie out to where her car was idling. I looked through the window to the garage again. Along the back wall stood a line of trucks. I shut my eyes, then opened them again to make sure I wasn't seeing a mirage.

It was still there—a pickup covered with orange primer. I caught my breath, then turned to the other window. I could see Rollie clicking my automatic lock, bending over it, listening. I looked at the pickup again. The noise of a grinding engine pervaded the office.

"You like old trucks?" I suddenly heard behind me. I looked at Rollie, flustered.

"Sorry," he said, pointing to my car. "It's about a two-hour job. I don't have that much time. Have to go somewhere tonight."

I nodded. "The Midwinter Festival, right?"

"Right."

"I learned all about it," I said. "But I've never been to one. Must be a lot of fun."

"Yeah. When do you want to bring her in?"

"Who?"

"The minivan."

"Oh. I don't know. I'll have to check with my dad."

"Okay." He put down the book.

"Look," I said. "I have another problem. I wonder if you can help me."

Frowning, Rollie turned back to me.

"It's about a social studies project," I said, suddenly feeling very foolish. "I'm supposed to be following someone around to learn about your school and all."

Rollie didn't say anything.

"But she seems to have disappeared," I said, "and I still have to do this report. I wonder if I could ask you a few questions. Like compare your BOCES garage with the one at my school?"

Rollie sat down on the corner of his desk.

"Shoot!"

"Thanks. First off, I see you do paint jobs and everything."

"That's right. You have something you want painted?"

"No. But—"

"You want to know if that pickup out there is the one that tried to mow down Paula Ash?"

Heart pounding, I stammered, "How did you—"

"My cousin Jimmy Cloud called me yesterday.

He told me she was there with him."

I caught my breath. "Is she okay?"

Rollie nodded. "She is for now. She told Jimmy about what happened to her. Told him about you."

Paula was okay! I closed my eyes and thanked God, then turned back to Rollie. I had a million questions for him, but Rollie wasn't having any just then.

"What if I told you that someone borrowed that truck Monday night?" he asked.

I bit my lip. "Do you know who?"

Rollie shook his head. "All I know is that whoever it was didn't have to break in. He had a key."

"Then it had to be one of the guys who worked here," I exclaimed.

"No, I checked that out."

I stared at him and did some quick pilpul. One, the guy who borrowed the truck didn't break in. Two, he had a key. Three, Rollie said that he'd checked out the BOCES people, and it wasn't any of them. Four, could someone have wanted to make it look like BOCES guys were guilty?

"Who else could get hold of a key to your garage?" I asked.

"Anyone waiting in here alone could have helped himself." Rollie pointed to a row of cubbyholes on the wall to his right. "My guys empty their pockets of everything, including their keys, before starting work and take their things back at night. It's a safety rule. So loose junk don't fall into the machinery."

"Was anyone's key missing that night?"

"No one mentioned it."

I looked at the keys in the cubbyholes. It wouldn't take long to get a duplicate key made. Someone in for a few hours of work might not wait around. Someone could easily snatch a key and then put back the original when they returned to get their car.

"Who came in for a short repair that day?" I asked.

Rollie laughed. "You kidding me? Kids, teachers, and townies are in and out of here all the time."

"But you have your appointment book, don't you?"

Rollie shook his head. "Not that one, I don't." He picked up the black book on the desk. "This one here is new. Yesterday afternoon, Lieutenant Jemison busted in here like a hurricane. He looked at the pickup, grilled us all like crazy, and left with my book. Next thing I knew, a crew of detective types was here going over that tin can for over an hour. Where he got wind of the pickup party, I don't know."

"I told him," I said. "I had to. I was so

worried about Paula."

Rollie put his hands in his pockets and paced the room, then came back to the desk.

"So what's it to you if Paula gets hurt?"

Suddenly, I recalled how he'd cut off my questions about Paula. How he had answered my question, "Is she okay?" with the words, "She is for now." I stared at him, terrified, imagining Paula in a dark room somewhere. Tied up. Tortured.

"What have you done with her?" I whispered. "What are you looking for, ransom?"

"Ransom?" Rollie threw back his head and laughed. "That would be like the *Ransom of Red Chief.*"

"The *Ransom of Red Chief?*" I'd read that story in English class. It was about a kidnapping. And the child the kidnappers snatched was so much trouble that they paid his parents a ransom to take him back.

"Paula's with Jimmy," Rollie said. "And I want her out of there! All she is for him is trouble. And just for the record, it wasn't Jimmy driving that pickup. Jimmy can't even drive—he's half blind."

Blind? "But he's supposed to be such a hotshot with the bow," I protested.

Rollie smiled. "Yeah. The elders say he sees with his ears. Look, no one forced Paula to run to him. That was her idea."

"I know," I said. "Paula must have been scared. I guess she told you that someone trashed the photography lab yesterday. I think it was whoever ran her into that ditch. I think he wants her film so bad he'd kill for it. *And* kill whoever might know who he is. At least with Jimmy she's safe."

Rollie frowned. "Not as safe as you think. She's got to get away before the trouble starts. Don't you see? She'll only make things worse."

"What trouble?"

"The Militia of God. They're saying Jimmy murdered Mindy Solomon. They're threatening an old-fashioned lynching. As if we'd do anything to hurt the Solomon family."

"Someone threw a brick into his window," I said. "He called Mr. Solomon a daughter-killer. They want the police to run him out of town."

"I hope not. Moshé is the best thing we have going at the garage. He gives us his overflow repair work. And he teaches us things."

Mr. Solomon here—with the keys and the truck! Well, that figured. "So Mr. Solomon spends a lot of time here?"

"Sure does," Rollie said. "But if Moshé starts believing those rumors Bill Hansen is spreading about us Seneca, it will ruin our garage. It's mostly all Seneca who work here. And he hires lots of guys from here when they graduate from high school." He balled his hand into a fist. "Ever since the end of the land lease, when their folks had to start paying rents, those jerks have been spoiling for a fight. Jimmy is just a scapegoat for them."

"Why are they using him?"

"Who knows? Maybe the scholarship. Maybe because he runs rings around them with the bow. Maybe it's just his roots. They can't stand that he's into Gai'wiio like the rest of us."

"What's that?"

"The religion of Handsome Lake."

"Is that up in Hiawartha Rocks?"

"It's not a place. It's a person, Ganioda'yo. Handsome Lake in English. He was a prophet back at the start of the nineteenth century. He set moral standards alongside our old beliefs. Folks called it the new religion. A lot of us are Christian also, but that's not good enough for the Militia of God. They can't stand that we also keep the old culture. Jimmy was split in half. You understand?"

"No. If this Militia of God was giving him such a hard time, why did he keep hanging with them? Why didn't he quit the archery club?"

Rollie's shoulders sagged. "It's Guthrie," he said. "He really likes Jimmy. He's the one who recommended Jimmy for that college scholarship. Four full years starting next September. And Jimmy's one of Guthrie's best archery instructors. He helps Guthrie teach the other kids bow holds. And he's in charge of all the archery stuff in the equipment room. Guthrie depends on him a lot. Jimmy doesn't want to let him down." His eyes blazed. "But this garbage has got to stop. Bill Hansen and his militia are warming up for trouble, and the word is they picked the first day of the Midwinter Festival. Well, this time the Gai'wiio Warriors will be waiting for them. And we don't need a white girl there so that Hansen's militia can tell the world they were out to save her honor."

"What's wrong with you guys? Didn't you ever hear of law and order and police?"

"Sure. Three weeks ago the Militia of God tried to blow up my aunt's clinic—and her with it. The police hauled the creeps in, and the judge let them out through the old revolving door. What did he care that they tried to kill Auntie? She took the proper precautions, seeing as how she knew that it was coming. But precautions or not, the only reason she's alive is that the grenade fizzled."

"She had predicted the attack?"

"Yeah, Auntie is like that. Well, this time, we're going to give those vigilantes a taste of old-time Seneca smoke. I hope Paula won't be there when it happens. I tried to convince her to leave, but she won't listen to me."

This is all my fault, I thought. I was the one who had convinced Paula to get the film developed. She had taken my advice, had gone to the lab, and had nearly gotten killed. Would she ever take advice from me again? I didn't know the answer but I knew it was worth a try. I looked at Rollie.

"I think she might listen to me," I said.

Rollie smiled at me. "You come with us and try, and I'll give you a *Ransom of Red Chief* deal."

"What do you mean?"

"Get Paula away from Jimmy, and I'll fix that car lock of yours for free."

chapter 15

My father looked up from his book. "Debbie Levine gave me your message. So the automatic lock is fixed?"

"No. We have to make a date with the guy at BOCES." I got some milk from the fridge and sipped it slowly, planning how to spring my decision to go to the Midwinter Festival on him. I was sure he was going to give me a hard time. But I couldn't put it off forever, could I? I finished my milk and took a breath. Then I blurted it all out. "We leave at noon," I finished.

"By all means go, Vivi," my father said. "It will be a great cultural experience. Make sure to take notes for your report. And don't worry about the driving. Just get me to the Solomons' tonight. Tomorrow, Shirley or her daughter, Lee, will take me anywhere I have to go."

That night, at the Solomon family's house, the two little girls tramped down the stairs and took my hands, each pulling me with her. Debbie was right. They certainly didn't seem like abused children.

"Your papa makes ten," Hendel said. "Ten men make a *minyan,* so now we can start the prayers." She danced me to the kitchen. "After the praying comes the food."

As we entered the large kitchen, I smelled the herring, fresh breads, noodle puddings, and honey cakes. The older, more reserved Rifka handed me a prayer book.

"Here's Mama," she said. I stood with other Jewish women from town, all of us in skirts or dresses. Shirley was there but not her daughter.

"Lee refused to come," Shirley told me. "Since her divorce problems, she is turned off by anything Orthodox."

Next to Shirley stood Moshé's wife, Malka. Her mouth looked grim as she held her baby. Whenever the baby cried, women would reach out their arms for him. They passed him around, cooed, and made him laugh.

"Magnified and sanctified be his great name—" We murmured the Hebrew prayers, out of view of the men who, respecting the

Orthodox household, did not look at us women while they prayed. It wasn't so bad—just different. But my best friend Rachael would never go for it. Or for Dov and Noah, the sons from Israel. They hovered near the table like two black shadows when the men finished praying and went to the buffet. It was spread with the food my father had brought from Buffalo. Mourners or not, the living must value life and take sustenance.

Like their parents, the sons wore slippers and sat on wooden orange crates to eat while friends and relatives comforted them. During the seven days of Shivah, the immediate family members over the age of thirteen would not leave the house lest they be distracted from their grief. They won't even wear shoes. They would not sit on soft chairs but only on these hard, wooden boxes to multiply their grief with discomfort. The two older sons were still sitting on the boxes and eating little cakes when I left.

thursday

chapter 16

My father set down his coffee. "Don't forget to call me when you get to Hiawartha Rocks. I don't know what kind of drivers these kids are."

"I'll be fine," I said with a lot more confidence than I felt. What did I know about these guys, after all?

"And call me before you're ready to leave."

"Oh, Dad," I sighed, hoping he would stop nagging. It was already eleven-thirty, and Rollie had said they were leaving at noon.

No other cars were parked outside the BOCES garage. I left the minivan and knocked warily at the door, wondering if they had left without me. The boy who opened it was an eighteenth-century apparition.

"Rollie?" I asked, staring at his buckskin leggings and breechcloth. His moccasins were beautifully decorated with porcupine quill embroidery.

Rollie laughed. "Hey, it's festival. What did you expect?"

I didn't know. I hadn't even thought about it—hadn't realized how important this festival was. Embarrassed by my ignorance, I stammered, "You look wonderful, Rollie. But where are the others? I thought we were taking off at noon."

"Indian time." He shrugged. "The last of them should be here by two." He handed me a zippered plastic clothing bag. "Put these on. The bathroom's in there. And be careful with them. They belonged to my grandmother's grandmother."

"A very important ancestor," another boy said. "Very smart like our aunt." I jumped at his voice. When had he slipped through the door?

"Auntie's too smart sometimes, Cousin," Rollie said, "She knows too much."

"Naturally," the other boy answered. "That's why she inherited the job."

"I thought your aunt was a doctor," I said. "Didn't she go to medical school?"

The boy nodded. "Of course. But medicine is

just one of her professions."

"What else does she do?"

"She's the matron of our clan," Rollie said. "Now stop the questions and get dressed. You'll be meeting her soon enough."

Me meet the clan matron? My heart skipped a beat. The clan matron wasn't just somebody's aunt. She was the keeper of all the clan names and titles, the person who selected people for religious and political positions.

I looked at Rollie. "How should I act? What should I do?"

"For starters, you can get into those clothes," he said.

The yellowed cotton blouse had once been white, I guessed. The buckskin skirt was stiff with age and heavy with intricate beadwork at the hem. It didn't quite make it down to the moccasins. That was okay—the moccasins didn't fit my long feet, so I would have to wear my boots. I put on the fur hat and the silver bracelet and looked around for a mirror. The one in the bathroom was too high up to see anything but my head, and the ones in the rest of the garage were hanging in cars. Pretty inconvenient for a once-over. All I could do was hope that I looked okay.

Praying I could get through the day without ripping or staining these valuable clothes, I walked stiffly back into the office. By one-fifteen, five guys had drifted in. If not for the fact that they were walking around, I would have thought they were figures in a museum display. Laughing and jostling, they all called each other "brother" or "cousin." The Iroquois had a lot of these, I remembered. All of a person's mother's sisters' kids and father's brothers' kids were considered to be sisters and brothers. The father's sisters' kids and the mother's brothers' kids were their cousins.

"You have a plan, Brother?" a boy asked.

"I have," Rollie answered. "Outside! We have to talk." I shivered, remembering their mission. Half an hour later, when they came back in, there were nine of them. Whatever they had to say, I guess they had their fill of talking. Once inside the truck, they didn't say anything until we'd been on the highway for an hour or more.

"Can you beat that? Another dead one!" a cousin said, pointing to the road ahead. Rollie's lips tightened as he swerved around the still deer. Then the soothing, swaying motion of the wheels stopped. Someone touched my shoulder. "We're here!"

"What time is it?" I asked, shaking myself awake.

"Festival time!" Rollie said. "Wow, the campground is packed."

That was a big help. I checked my watch.

Twenty after three. I climbed out of the truck and looked at the trailers, tents, minivans, and RVs, at the people setting up house, calling to one another, laughing. A baby howled. Dogs slept. A mother dragged a kid toward the public washroom.

Above it all rose a towering hill of pudding stone rock, studded with pebble and cobble. Over thousands of years, the rock had developed cracks that widened, forming huge rectangular blocks, which gravity gradually pulled down the hillside. As they slid, crevices widened into the alleys, streets, and chambers of the giant rock city that the Seneca had named Hiawartha Rocks.

A sign about thirty feet up read "No one past this point." Some kids were running beyond it and laughing.

"Brian! Evan! Get down here right now!" a woman called. "No one can go up there. It's too dangerous!"

Rollie looked at the others. "Okay, Cousins, you know the plan. Jimmy is expecting us after dark. The kids will be sleeping then, and the others will be too busy dancing to see anything. No one gets hurt."

"And Bill Hansen and friends?"

"They won't find the warrior hideout by themselves. Only problem is taking Vivi to Paula by daylight. When I take off with Vivi, make sure that Hansen's guys follow you."

"Where?"

"Wherever you want to take them."

"Like that cave on Big Bear Ridge?"

"Right!" Rollie laughed. "But before we do anything else, we must go pay our respects to Auntie. Leave the weapons here for now. And remember, use them only in defense." I followed them down the hill toward a clearing.

A blue jay screeched. Two does up ahead scattered. Squirrels and a rabbit scurried across my path. Above the animal sounds, a human voice boomed out.

"Our nephews and nieces!"

"Move it," Rollie said. "The bigheads are starting."

I looked up to see two men in buffalo robes and masks walking toward the clearing. Around their necks, they wore strings of corn husks. In the old days, I knew, the bigheads went from longhouse to longhouse announcing the start of the festival. I watched them walk into a structure in the middle of the clearing. About twenty feet wide and over fifty feet long, it looked like a giant felled tree.

The building was shingled with elm bark and its frame was made of logs set upright in the ground. Strips of the bark of a basswood tree fastened crosspoles to the frame every few feet. The curved roof was made of saplings bent across the structure and was shingled with elm bark. People were heading toward it, but not the ones wearing jeans and parkas—only the people in buckskin like us.

"Here we are," said Rollie. He pulled me toward a bark door surrounded by animal carvings. "Wolf," he said to a man with gold teeth and whispered in my ear, "Show him your bracelet."

I uncovered my wrist while the man studied me.

"She wears my grandmother's grandmother's clothes," Rollie said. The man smiled at him and then at me. I jerked Rollie's arm.

"What was that all about?"

"Shush," he whispered. "It's just clan ID. Each clan used to have a longhouse. This one's for everyone now. We use it for meetings and religious stuff. Only clan members are allowed inside for religious things." I turned toward the door, but Rollie grabbed my arm. "Hey, I have to pay respects to my aunt. Where are you going?"

"Out of here! It would be great to meet your aunt, but I don't belong."

Rollie tightened his grasp. "Sure you do. The old man at the door thinks we're engaged."

"Engaged?" I stared at him. Rollie pointed to my clothes.

"Yeah, that's what he thinks. Why else would I let you wear those? I couldn't leave you out there with Bill Hansen's creeps around, could I?"

The longhouse was wall-to-wall with people and smelled of wood smoke. In front of a hearth stood the two men in buffalo robes and masks.

"Our nephews and nieces," the taller one called three times, "Now the ceremony of all the great riddle has begun. Now moreover he who lives upwards where there is an earth in the sky, he who is our maker and has given it to us, he has made our bodies tremble. And you who are chiefs, and also you officials, and also our mothers, and moreover the young people, and also you children—now all of you shall stand firm."

"He's not as good an actor as the bighead we had last year," Rollie whispered. I leaned forward to get a better view of the bighead. He seemed pretty kosher to me.

"Now the smoke arises from where the officials have kindled a fire, and it reaches even to the heavens, for the Holder-of-the-Heavens has decreed that the ceremony should be performed on earth as in the Sky World."

The tall bighead stepped back, and the shorter one came forward and spoke.

"Now moreover all of you shall attend the ceremonies where the officials have built a fire. Everyone must go there, even the children, and you old people shall lead them by the hand, for now the Dream Rite has commenced. Therefore if one has a new dream and also a particular dream, that person shall fulfill all of the old dreams, and it is urgent that that person reveal any new dreams or else she or he might become ill, for whoever fails to renew his dreams and reveal new dreams brings trouble to the community."

Four masked, robed men clicked their turtle shell rattles. Rollie touched my arm. "The medicine men," he explained.

"And for that," the bighead continued, "the matron of the house will be responsible, for the matron of the house knows who has had dreams and who will be to blame."

Nine grandmother types and one slim, dark-haired woman, all in elaborate buckskin like mine, stepped forward. Each wore a pendant carved with a different animal.

"Wait here!" Rollie said, "I'll be right back." He walked toward the younger woman with the wolf symbol dangling from her neck. They spoke for what seemed a long while. From time to time, he pointed to me.

"Who's that?" I asked, when he returned.

"My aunt," he answered.

The woman smiled and waved to me. People got up and stretched. The longhouse was emptying out. We were walking toward the door when Rollie's aunt touched his shoulder, then held out her hand to me.

"Stay for the Dream Rite, both of you," she said. "Since we've invited some guests who are not of our Iroquois people, I'm afraid we must hold it outside." She pointed to a group of young people seated on one of two benches, which faced each other. "Look, there are your favorite cousins in the moiety."

Moiety. I knew I had learned about it in social studies, but I could not remember what it meant.

"What's a moiety?" I asked Rollie. He didn't answer. His mouth tightened as he dragged me toward the bench where the cousins moved closer together and made room for us.

"What's a moiety?" I whispered to the cousin nearest me, but he wasn't talking either. He was staring at the kids in jeans and parkas who, led by Bill Hansen, were walking toward the bench facing us. Two masked medicine men followed them, clicking their turtle shell rattles.

"My nephews and nieces," said the tall bighead, "today is a special day, for on this day we shall entertain guests, and you shall know that hospitality is one of our great virtues."

"What's going on?" one of the cousins asked. "We never had strangers at the Dream Rite before."

Rollie winked at me as he said, "Of course

not! They're not allowed in the longhouse. That's why they're having it outside."

"Now listen closely, for the rules are thus: A person in one moiety will speak a dream to the hearers in that moiety. Then all but one hearer shall be silent, but that one shall speak unto the opposite moiety and hint as to the substance of the dream. Moreover, it is essential for the opposite moiety to guess the dream lest the people fall ill and bring harm to the community. For this the matron of this house, the Wolf Matron, will bear all responsibility."

I looked at Rollie's aunt, but she was smiling and didn't seem worried at all, as if holding the rite outside didn't matter.

Rollie looked at her, too. "Oh, no," he said. "She's done me again."

"My nephews and nieces, my nephews and nieces, my nephews and nieces," sang the bigheads. "Let the riddles begin."

The cousins got into a huddle. Then Rollie walked toward the other bench. "It is not a ball, yet you throw it," he said. No response.

"Its voice is like thunder." Silence. Rollie scratched his head.

"What sees, it makes blind, what hears, it makes deaf, what breathes, it strangles." Rollie waited, but no one guessed. He narrowed his eyes.

"What brings life, it would bring death."

"Liar!" shouted Bill Hansen. "She kills

babies! The dream is about a grenade. Too bad ours was a dud."

"It hides in a cave," Bill Hansen said.

"A bear," called a cousin.

Bill Hansen shook his head. "It hunts without sight."

"A bat," Rollie said.

Hansen frowned. "Its kill is young and white. But we will stop him forever later tonight."

Rollie spat. "Over my dead body."

"Maybe," Hansen said.

"Guess the dream," said the Wolf Matron.

Rollie shrugged. "It's about Jimmy Cloud."

"Five points for each moiety," said the tall bighead, and he nodded to the medicine men. "Our visitors are taking their leave now." The medicine men led them away.

A few bigheads followed the cousins, too. Rollie and I turned to leave, but the Wolf Matron blocked our path.

"Wait, Nephew," she said. "The bigheads would like to meet you and your friend." She steered us gently but firmly toward the bigheads.

"Greeting, Uncles," Rollie said. "I am Rolland Hawkes. This is Aviva Hartman. She wears my grandmother's grandmother's dress."

"Greetings, Nephew," said the tall bighead. "I

am William Jemison. This is my deputy Roger Sands. We wear the badge of the Pikes County Tribal Police. At the moment, some of my officers, dressed as medicine men, are detaining Bill Hansen and the rest of you hoods. If you don't want your butt in jail for the rest of the festival, you'll lead me to Jimmy Cloud's hiding place."

"Right now?"

"I wish we could," the policeman said. "Doc said the boy needs his insulin, but leaving in daylight, someone would spot us for sure. We'd have more kids from the festival tailing us than the Pied Piper. With the parents taking off after them, all hell would break loose." The lieutenant shook his head. "It's only a couple of hours till dark. My gut says it is better to wait."

chapter 17

They didn't strangle the white dog in the longhouse but outside in the crisp, fresh air. They prettied him up with paint and strings of white wampum, then hung him by the neck from an eight-foot-high pole. As back in the ancient times, they didn't spill one drop of blood. This white dog didn't have any blood— just that straw stuffing they put into toys.

"How long will they leave it there?" I asked.

"All eight days," the young deputy said. He had changed out of the bighead costume and stood straight and tall in his crisp gray uniform. "Stupid, isn't it? In the old days it was even worse. They used a real dog."

Rollie glared at him and took my arm. "Excuse us, Auntie," he said to the Wolf

Matron. "We want to go watch the lacrosse."

I pulled my arm away. "What will happen to the toy dog in the end?"

The deputy shrugged, but the Wolf Matron spoke. "The Creator has a dream, the same one each year. He dreams of a guardian against the dangers of the year ahead. By the end of eight days, the people shall guess his dream."

The deputy tapped his moccasin. "Oh, Wolf Matron, spare us. You don't really believe all this, do you?"

The Wolf Matron ignored him. "Then we'll place the white dog in the flames on the altar, along with the sacred tobacco, and send him up to the Sky World. He will be our messenger to the Great Spirit. The white dog will assure the Great Spirit of our loyalty and thank him for the blessings of the year."

She fastened hard eyes on the deputy. "It's important that we do this every year so future generations will not forget their spiritual heritage."

The deputy sighed and turned to me. "I guess you think we're pretty primitive, don't you?"

"Oh, I don't know," I said. "My tribe used to send up a roasted lamb at Passover."

"But you don't do it now, do you?"

I shook my head. "No. Now we use a roasted shank bone."

The festival vendors were doing a brisk business. People crowded around booths selling silver jewelry, carved wooden trinkets, bright woven blankets, and wonderful-smelling food. The deputy and I ate ice cream bars and cheered the Wolf Team in the lacrosse game. Rollie sat and sulked

"I think I'll try some snow snake," he said after a while.

"Just don't try anything funny," the deputy warned him as the three of us trudged to the snow-snake track. "I'm armed, you know."

People lined both sides of the snow-packed alley. "Well, Rollie Hawkes, you ready to throw?" the starter challenged.

Rollie tossed me his coat and walked to the head of the track. He picked up a giant log, his muscles straining under the weight. Slowly, he raised it high then flung it forward. I held my breath as the log touched down and sped across the snow. People cheered as it sailed, slowed, and stopped.

A man down the track raised a flag and shouted something that I couldn't hear. I stamped my feet against the cold as the words came back up the line. "Forty-one yards."

"Good throw!" said the starter. The deputy pursed his lips.

"How about you, Roger Sands?" the starter asked. The deputy looked at the starter, then at Rollie. The starter pointed to the logs. "Well?"

"I'll hold your jacket," I said. But the deputy

handed his jacket to the starter, then looked at us and patted his shoulder holster. The day's last rays of sunlight glinted off his gun as he threw.

"What do you know?"

"How about that?"

"He got the same distance!"

"Good throwing!" the starter said. "You each get twenty points for your moiety."

There was that word again, and I still couldn't remember what it meant.

"What's a moiety?" I asked.

"Forget it!" the deputy said.

"I want to know."

"Then ask him." The deputy pointed to Rollie. "He goes in for all that garbage."

Rollie winced and kicked a piece of ice. "I'm cold. Let's go inside and watch Auntie do the baby naming."

The longhouse was warm with fires. We sat on a bench, and Rollie ate fried bread and beans. The deputy got a hamburger. I unwrapped a Swiss cheese sandwich I'd brought from home, and we watched the baby naming. Toddlers were running around making noise.

"This is a very good name," the Wolf Matron said to a young woman holding a baby. "This man died only last month and released it. He worked hard and was good to his family."

"We give kids Hebrew names after the dead,

too," I said to the deputy and Rollie.

"Terrific!" said the deputy. "You're as Stone Age as us." Rollie didn't say anything. I don't think he heard me above the racket the older children were making.

The clan matron looked at some of the toddlers and shook her head. "You children are very bad. I shall have to call Longnose, the cannibal clown." She nodded to someone in robes and a long-nosed mask.

The toddlers squealed as if in fear, then laughed and ran. Rollie looked at the deputy. "We still have a little time to kill. How about a go at the bowl game?"

The deputy shrugged. We walked through the longhouse to a table with a lot of people around it. Deputy Sands reached in his pocket and pulled out some change. We pushed our way to a bent old man who was giving out bowls.

"Last one," he said. "Play fast. We quit at nightfall." He set a bowl down on a table. Rollie and the deputy sat down on facing benches. Rollie pulled the wooden bowl toward him. Inside the bowl were five chips, black on one side and red on the other.

"One parking permit for red," he said to Deputy Sands.

The deputy put back his change. He dug his hand into the bowl and mixed up the chips so some were red-side-up and some were black. Rollie tossed. Three chips came up black and two came up red. Rollie said, "You got me!"

"I can remember when we used painted peach pits," the bowl keeper said. "Now everything's plastic."

The deputy took the bowl. "One oil change for black," he said and tossed. Four chips came up red and only one black. "That's life," he said.

Six throws later, Rollie had won a one-hour special parking permit, a front seat voucher for the Policeman-Fireman Baseball game, and a ticket to the policemen's ball. The deputy had two oil changes and a wheel alignment. "Give someone else a turn," a woman said.

"You want to play all night, get the software," a kid hollered.

"Time's up," the bowl keeper said. "Six points each for your moieties."

"What's a moiety?" I asked him.

The old man grimaced. "You kids these days don't know anything. Don't you remember the legend about the twins?"

I shook my head.

The bowl keeper sighed. "At the beginning of the world, there were these two twins, you know? One was left-handed and one was right-handed. They competed with each other all the time—in the bowl game, lacrosse, snow snake, you name it."

"Who won?" I asked him.

The bowl keeper shrugged. "It was a draw. They each lent balance to the other. So together they accomplished wonderful things. See?"

"Not really."

The bowl keeper scratched his head. "It's because of the twins that each tribe is made up of two moieties. These moieties compete against each other in games, but on important problems they always work together, each using their skills for the good of the tribe." The old man began collecting the bowls. "Hear those drums? It's getting black as pitch out there. Time to bed down the kids and start celebrating."

The deputy stood up. "Yup. Time to dance!" He grabbed Rollie's arm. "Come along. The lieutenant is waiting for us."

chapter 18

The lieutenant looked up at the rocks, then back at us. "All set, Auntie?"

The Wolf Matron pointed to her medical bag. "I have insulin in case his level is low and glucose if it's too high. I hope we won't need either of them."

"How far up do we have to walk?" asked the deputy. "It's a pretty cold night."

Jemison frowned. "Just keep moving, Roger."

"Yes," said the Wolf Matron. "Look at those dancers down there. As long as they keep dancing, they won't get hypothermia."

And then we were leaving the fires and the dancers behind us, climbing past the sign that read, "No one past this point," skirting the ridges. Did women once hike in these stiff buckskin skirts? I would have preferred jeans myself. I was thankful for the fur hat, though. Now that the sun was gone, it was cold. As my boots crunched the thin layer of snow, I was glad the Iroquois moccasins hadn't fit.

A doe stared at the beam of my flashlight, then moved on to more interesting things. I looked up at the rock city, at the clouds that hid the stars, and then at Rollie, who was leading us to Jimmy's secret hideout.

For almost half an hour, he and Lieutenant Jemison had talked. By the time they finished, it seemed to me that Rollie had done a complete turnaround. "The lieutenant's plan is pretty neat," he told me. "They'll bring Jimmy in, but only to question him and keep him safe from angry mobs while the police go after the real killer."

"So Lieutenant Jemison doesn't think it's Jimmy?" I asked.

"Right. I told you Jimmy didn't do it."

I shrugged. "Sure, but he's your friend. Why does Lieutenant Jemison think he's innocent?"

"Because Jimmy's a Seneca."

"Seneca don't commit murder?"

"Not in the sacred places. That field used to be a favorite hunting place in the old days. It's where most of our fathers and grandfathers were taught to use the bow. They said it was one of the first places the Sky Woman saw when she looked down through the hole in the sky at our world."

"The world on the back of the turtle?"

Rollie smiled. "Right. How did you know that?"

"I had to learn your story of creation for social studies class. Is that why a Seneca wouldn't commit murder there?"

"Exactly. Of course, there are other good hunting places the elders say that about, but there's also another reason. The tall grass where they found her? Jimmy would never have been in that field."

"Why is that?"

"When the engineers blasted the hole for the dam, a lot of animals had to find new homes. That high grass where Mindy was lying became a neighborhood for poisonous snakes. No Seneca in his right mind would go in there."

"So Jemison must think it's one of the town kids?"

"I guess. Although I don't know of any kid who'd know his way there and back. Ever since the trouble over building the dam, we haven't let townies hunt on that side of the creek."

"And before that you did?"

Rollie nodded. "But that was over thirty years ago. In the old days, we let them hunt a lot further inside our land—as long as they stayed out of the sacred places. Only Iroquois could hunt there."

Jemison signaled for Rollie to come ahead. He waved to me and ran to catch up with the lieutenant.

I was glad to be alone. I needed to do some pilpul. So what did I have? One, the townies once hunted deep inside Indian land, but they had to avoid the sacred places. Two, if they had to avoid them, they would have to know where those sacred places were. Three, it was more than thirty years since townies had hunted that deep into Indian land. Over thirty years ago, the archery kids hadn't even been born. Four, Mindy's killer must be someone older. Moshé Solomon? Mindy's father had lived in town as a boy. He must be old enough to have hunted thirty years ago. Five, Rollie had said Mr. Solomon gave BOCES a lot of his overflow work. Was part of that overflow the truck that ran Paula off the road?

At least another hour went by before Rollie held up his hand. "Here's the opening," he whispered. "It's low, so watch your head. The room is further back. You have to crawl until you get to the archway that leads into the big cave."

Jemison bellied through the crack, his lantern playing against the walls. The doctor was at his heels, the rest of us behind. The tunnel widened as I snaked the ground. The odor of a banked fire clogged my nostrils.

"Jimmy!" the policeman shouted, "It's Lieutenant Jemison."

Nothing.

Jemison turned and beckoned to me. "Call Paula," he whispered. Heart thumping, I moved forward. My hair got caught on something jagged. I jerked it free.

"Paula," I called, "It's me, Vivi. We have to talk."

I listened. No sound. Oh, God, had they left this place?

"For Christ's sake, Jimmy, get out here!" yelled the deputy. "We'll get the truth out of you in the end!"

In the darkness before us, the silence was deafening.

"Quiet, Roger!" Jemison whispered. "You'll scare him half to death." He inched forward. "Is Paula with you, Jimmy?"

"I'm here," Paula called. "Don't hurt him. Please. He's sick."

"We won't hurt anyone. Listen to me, Jimmy," Jemison shouted. "Rollie Hawkes led us here. You trust him, don't you?" He waited.

Rollie squirmed past the lieutenant. "Look, Jimmy, Jemison's okay. He knows you didn't do it. He'll protect you and Paula while we find the real killer."

"Killer, killer, killer," a voice sang out from the dark. "Killer, they'll call me."

Rollie shouted. "You didn't kill anyone, Jimmy Cloud! We know that! And you don't need to hide in the dark like some old mole."

"I'll kill you, paleface. Watch out!" the voice called.

Rollie moved forward. "Paleface? Me? You crazy, Jimmy?"

"Be careful, Rollie," the Wolf Matron whispered. "Jimmy sounds disoriented. He could be going into diabetic shock."

Rollie nodded and slithered into the archway. I saw an arrow fly toward him and land at his feet.

"Don't come any closer, paleface. I have you covered," called Jimmy.

Rollie stood up. "So shoot me," he challenged. "And if you get your butt out of here alive, good luck finding a friend as true as me."

I heard a rifle blast and saw in the dim lantern light that the rock above Rollie's head was crumbling. Rollie jumped aside and grabbed a handful of shards as they fell.

"So it's guns now! My turn, Cousin!" Rollie called. He leaped into the darkness. "Gotcha!"

The Wolf Matron felt for a pulse then reached into her bag. "Just sugar, Jimmy," she said and jabbed the needle into his vein.

I looked at Paula. "You okay?"

"I'm okay," she answered. "Just scared. Rollie got to Jimmy just before he hit the ground."

"The glucose should help," the Wolf Matron said, spreading the bright woven blanket over her patient.

Paula smoothed a lock of Jimmy's dark hair off his forehead. "What's wrong with him, doctor?"

The Wolf Matron sighed. "I'm afraid he's in insulin shock. Too much insulin. Not enough food."

I looked around the cave, wondering if there was enough of anything. Two sleeping bags lay on the ground on either side of a carton. Judging by the candles and tissue box on top, I guessed that it served as a nightstand. Taped to the granite wall was a photo of the dam, like the one in Paula's house. Books and *Seneca Nation* magazines littered the ground like small rugs. A crate near the camp stove appeared empty.

Rollie plopped down on the bedroll and looked from the crate to Paula. "What happened to our stock of three sisters?"

"I dumped them. Those veggies were older than I am." She turned to the doctor. "All we had left today was a bag of pretzels."

"He won't be in any condition to walk for quite a while. Since we can't get an ambulance up these trails, you men will have to carry him," said the Wolf Matron.

Lieutenant Jemison walked back toward the archway and spoke into his phone. "Copter is on its way," he said when he returned. "The going will be a bit slow, but we should make it down by midnight."

"Midnight?" I whispered to Paula. "Yikes! If my father hasn't heard from me by midnight, he'll call every hospital in town."

"That's easy," she said. "There's only one."

A cloud drifted in front of the moon. The procession stopped while Jemison shifted his part of Jimmy to Rollie. Paula shined her flashlight at the "No one past this point" sign.

"Look at those two idiots!" she said. "They can't read."

"Where are they?" shouted the deputy, patting his holster. He pointed his flashlight at two figures, now on the next higher ridge. Their black coats flared as they disappeared into a crevice between some boulders.

I shivered, wondering why they had looked so familiar, and glanced down at the campground below. Some fires had gone out, while others still burned. Beside them, a number of Seneca lay sprawled. as if exhausted. Others sat talking or eating, but most were still dancing when the blast silenced the drums and the rock fragments hurtled toward them like missiles.

chapter 19

The hall of the hospital was crowded when they brought me in and plopped me down. My cheek hurt. When I touched it, it felt fat and swollen. "It looks like a bad bruise," the nurse said. "The doctor will check you out for fractures later. She's got worse cases to see to right now."

On the stretcher next to me, I saw Jimmy. I looked around frantically. "Where's Paula?"

Jimmy sighed. "At the police station. The lieutenant thinks she'll be safe there. Glad you're okay. A hunk of rock must have bounced up and got you." The serious look in his eyes and determined set of his chin were softened by a friendly, crooked-toothed smile. "I heard someone say that the bombers used dynamite."

Dynamite? What was it Lieutenant Jemison had said the other night? Moshé Solomon had been using dynamite to blast the hole for his used car lot. I saw in my mind his long, black coat—the two black coats disappearing into the crevice seconds before the blast.

"Rollie's okay, too?" I asked.

"Yeah. Jemison deputized him. He's up hunting skunk with Roger Sands. Hope they bag those creeps."

I thought about the twins who competed against each other, yet who could work together for the good of the tribe. "I hope so, too," I said. An ambulance siren screamed, then abruptly stopped. I looked at Jimmy. "How many—"

"A lot of broken bones and stuff. No one dead so far. Could be, though, before the night is over. One guy is touch and go."

Lieutenant Jemison was walking toward us, his face grim. A camera flashed. Someone thrust a mike at Jimmy. "You, kid. You're Jimmy Cloud, aren't you? Where were you at the time of the explosion?"

"You're out of here," the lieutenant hissed at the newsman. He shooed the guy away and turned to Jimmy. "Someone wants to see you."

"Oh? Who?"

"Mr. Guthrie." Jimmy clenched his fists.

Lieutenant Jemison continued, "Doc said

he'd have to wait until tomorrow," Jimmy's hands relaxed. Jemison looked at him and asked, "The kids said he called you 'Straight Arrow.' That right? You some kind of teacher's pet?"

Jimmy's nostrils flared. "He likes people who are good at things. He gave us names to show it."

Jemison nodded. "What were some of the others?"

"Avery with his piano playing is 'Chopin.'"

"And Bill Hansen?" Jemison asked.

Jimmy shrugged. "Mr. Guthrie calls him 'Buffalo Bill.'"

"Did he have nicknames for the girls?"

"Just her."

"Mindy Solomon?"

"Yeah."

"What did he call her?"

"Snow White."

Jemison raised his eyebrows. "What did he say she was good at?"

"Purity."

"And was she good at that, Jimmy?"

"How the hell should I know?" He shut his eyes but the tears dripped out. "I didn't kill her—even if my fingerprints were all over her."

"We know," Jemison said.

Jimmy's eyes narrowed. "How?"

"By the looks of it, Mindy put up quite a fight. We found blood and skin under her fingernails, like she scratched her assailant. Your aunt helped with the autopsy. She takes samples of your blood regularly to test for sugar levels, doesn't she?"

"She's always jabbing me. So what?"

"Once you ran away, the Wolf Matron predicted the rest. She knew the militia would try to hang it on you. She knew they'd go after Paula, too. It's unreal how that woman knows what's coming. It's like she has a direct line to the Great Spirit." Jemison lowered his voice. "I'm convinced she knew what we would find in that autopsy, because even before the coroner was done the doctor sent us a medical file on you. No way could you be the killer, not with the blood type you have." Jemison put an arm around Jimmy's shoulder. "So now are you ready to tell me why you went into the snake pit and then ran?"

Jimmy pursed his lips. "I guess."

"Good," Jemison said. He looked down the corridor where a TV camera crew was interviewing a guy with a head bandage. "For now, we're letting folks think what they want, like maybe we have the murderer. Meanwhile, we'll take you down to the jailhouse where we can talk. You'll be safe there."

And the killer will think he's the one who's safe, I thought.

"How long will I have to stay?" Jimmy

asked, frowning.

Jemison sighed. "That depends on what you can tell me." The policeman pushed some buttons on his cell phone. "Anything, Roger?" he asked. "Too bad. Well, wrap it up for the night. Leave a few men out there and get the Hawkes kid home." He slammed the phone shut as the TV crew moved toward us.

"Hey there, lieutenant," a cameraman yelled, "You taking him in or what?"

Jemison grinned. "You bet your life!" He turned to Jimmy. "Time to put the cuffs on, kid," he whispered. "You up to kicking and screaming for the press?"

"Hospital?" my father shouted. "She's in the hospital," he said to someone else.

"I'm fine, Dad, really. Just a bruise on the cheek."

"Is Paula with you?"

"No, but she's okay. One person is critical but there's no one dead, thank God. An awful lot of people are injured. Oh, Dad, the Wolf Matron was wonderful."

"Who?"

"The doctor. The medics from Raven's Peak were here, too. And the air rescue team out of Buffalo flew down. I can't believe you didn't hear about it, Dad. The TV cameras were all over the place."

"I didn't watch any TV tonight. Look, ya-keerati, I'll have someone drive me right down to get you."

"But Dad, the lieutenant arranged for a po-liceman to drive me. He even sent someone to pick up the minivan from the BOCES garage."

Dad's voice was muffled. "She has a ride." There was a pause. "Okay," he said to me, "ask him to bring Paula along with you."

"I can't."

"Is she hurt?" my father asked.

"Oh, my God, she's hurt!" a woman's voice cried out.

"No, Dad. She's at the jailhouse." I heard the catch of breath and said, "For her protection."

My father's voice turned gentle. "She's okay, Lee. Turn on the news."

Two hours later, the doctor let me leave. A policewoman drove me home along Main Street, past the shut-down stores with the metal grillwork in front of the glass to discour-age intruders. I thought about my father help-ing Lee Ash get her religious divorce. But wasn't she visiting awfully late?

"It's all your fault, Mom," I shouted silently. "You were the one who left!" I covered my face and sobbed.

"Go ahead, cry," the policewoman said. "You've earned it. It's been a rough day."

friday

chapter 20

The alarm at my bedside rang at seven. I turned over and yawned, ready to go back to sleep again. Why bother to go up to the high school when Paula wouldn't be there to follow around? Then I remembered why I had set my clock. I had to call Rachael before she left for school. I dragged myself downstairs to the phone and dialed her number in Buffalo. "I have a favor to ask," I said, then spoke fast.

"Of course I'll do it," she told me. "I'll be at Hebrew school this afternoon anyway. I'll stop into the temple library before my four o'clock class. It shouldn't take long to look up what you want. I'll call you back about three forty-five, okay?"

I thanked her and went back to bed, but

tired as I was, I couldn't sleep. I kept thinking about last night, wondering what the reaction was at the school. For the second time that morning, I pulled myself out of bed. There was no way to know but to go there and find out.

The back door to Pikes Landing Central was locked. I walked around to the front through slushy tire tracks, dodging a snowball. The boy who threw it didn't mean it for me. He'd aimed the projectile of love at a blonde with a red stocking cap. She ducked it and laughed, then ran toward the flagpole where a bunch of kids stood singing, "Christmas tree, O Christmas tree."

Aaron Kaplan and Bill Hansen were among them. According to Debbie Levine, Bill had led the searchers right to Mindy's body. If Bill Hansen had murdered Mindy, he must be feeling very safe—back at school and free, with Jimmy locked up in jail for the crime.

I looked at Aaron. He was out of jail, too. But at the service my father would hold tonight, I knew we couldn't count on Aaron for the minyan. If only the rabbi hadn't had to leave and the temple still held services and had a Hebrew school, maybe a kid like Aaron wouldn't have drifted away from his roots. A wave of sadness washed over me as I pushed past the singers to the door.

The halls were buzzing as usual, but not a

single Seneca was around. For the kids who clogged the corridors, there was only one topic of the day. Over and over, I heard the words "injured" and "dead" and the names "Jimmy" and "Paula."

At the door to homeroom, Josh Levy caught up with me. "Hard to believe Paula was in on it," he said. "All this talk about her being jealous because Mindy was having Jimmy's baby is pretty darn hard to believe."

"You bet," I said. "It's really crazy. The coroner didn't find any sign of pregnancy."

"He wasn't even Mindy's type," said Josh.

I looked at him. "Who was?"

Josh frowned. "You know, those holy rollers. Like Bill Hansen." He shook his head. "When I think what a pothead he was back in middle school. But Billy Boy's been straight as a ruler since Guthrie gathered him in. Best quarterback on the team, too."

"So Bill and Mindy were a thing?"

Josh shrugged. "Once she started going to that Bible group, she came to all the Friday night games. Doesn't take much to figure out why, does it?"

What I was trying to figure was how Mindy Solomon got past her family on Friday night, the Sabbath. I wasn't allowed to go anywhere but to temple. What drove her to go? The Christian Bible class or one of the people in it?

"What about last Friday night?" I asked. "The night before she died? Was she there at the game?"

"Sat right up front, as usual."

"Did she look any different, like she was scared or upset?"

"I didn't look at her so close. All I know is when we came out of the locker room, she was waiting for Bill. Then they left."

"You know where they went?"

"To the Bible meeting. Where else? That's where they went after all the games. Hansen was in a huff. He didn't say a word to the rest of us."

"Why was that?"

Josh shrugged. "I guess because Saunders, the tight end, got that knee injury. Bill was on our backs every practice, trying to get the whole team to those Bible meetings. Friday night we were up against the Cayuga Creek team. Their guys are twice the size of most of us. After practice the night before, Hansen started badgering us like always. Said Coach Guthrie asked us to pray that no one got hurt in the game."

"What did you do?"

"Said I was going home. Most of the others did the same. Except for Bobby O'Donnell."

"What did he do?"

"He looked Hansen straight in the eye. 'Sure,

Bill,' he said, 'praying that no one gets hurt is a great idea. Let's all go down to my church, St. Gregory's, and say some Hail Marys.' We thought it was funny. And then the next night, Saunders got hurt. Hansen was blazing that night."

"What about Mr. Guthrie? Was he angry?"

"Heck, no. He's cool."

Most of the teachers didn't even try to teach. Some let us talk quietly and visit, while warbling carolers walked in and out of the rooms. That's why I was kind of surprised when Mr. Guthrie's English class was business as usual. Ignoring the noise from the corridors and restlessness of his students, he assigned us a reading from *Hamlet* and a paragraph on the quote, "Conscience makes cowards of us all."

"Hand it in at the end of class," he said. When I brought mine up, he smiled at me, but his eyes looked sad. "Thank you, Ms. Hartman," he said. "I saw you speaking to Jimmy at the hospital. Do you think you will see him today?"

"I don't know," I answered.

"If you do," he said, "Please tell him I've been praying for him."

At lunch, the cafeteria was a mob scene. There was more food on the walls than on the tables with their abandoned trays. Kids were running in all directions while the monitors stood around and laughed. Then somebody yelled, "Here they come!"

I looked at the door. Into the bedlam marched a line of carolers, led by a kid in a Santa Claus costume and mask. "'Deck the Halls,'" they sang.

"'Twelve Days of Christmas,'" someone shouted.

The carolers obliged.

"'Silent Night!'" a listener yelled.

They sang until the bell rang, then marched out the door still singing. The corridor was a zoo. I turned toward the staircase, but the carolers carried me down the hall, past the pay phones, the wood shop, and the art room to the photo lab. The guy in the Santa suit was behind me. Suddenly, he pushed me against the door and stuck a key in the lock.

"Where did you get that key?" I whispered.

"Let's just say that I have faculty connections." He opened the door and shoved me inside. "You and I have to talk."

My hands went cold and clammy. "Who are you?"

He ripped off his mask and beard.

Bill Hansen! His face was haggard, his eyes red like he hadn't slept much. I wondered if he and his buddies were awake all night in jail, betting on the body count. Were they disappointed that no Seneca had been killed?

"What do you want with me?" I whispered, my voice hoarse with fright. But my fears subsided as his shoulders drooped.

"I want you to take a message to Jimmy."

I licked my dry lips. "Haven't you tried to hurt him and his people enough?"

Bill shook his head. "I don't pretend to love Indians, but we were in jail. No one can blame us for the explosion."

"Oh, no?" I asked. "Who spread the word that Mindy was killed by an Indian? Who marched around with signs to rile folks up? Whoever did it, you helped stir up the hate that made it happen."

Hansen didn't say anything.

"And what about this photo lab? I suppose you're going to tell me that you guys didn't trash it?"

"What? I don't know what you're talking about." He held out his hands. "Look, I brought you here just to ask you to tell Jimmy we're praying for him."

"Tell him yourself."

"He won't see me. But I want him to know that we pray for sinners."

"How kind of you," I said, growing more angry. "But what makes you so sure he's a sinner?"

Hansen smiled at me sadly, the way Mr. Guthrie had. "You're new around here. You don't know how they treat their own girls. It starts with a few drinks at one of their bashes. Then they beat them black-and-blue. Killing must get easier after that."

My words rushed out like a river I couldn't stop. "Does it? All Indian boys are killers, then? And the rest of you are lily white? Sorry, but I won't buy into your prejudice. And killing Mindy would have been a lot easier for you. It was you who took Mindy to all of those meetings, you she came to the games to see. You're wasting your time bad-mouthing Jimmy. The police have proof that he didn't do it!"

Hansen stared at me. "What proof?"

"Mindy scratched her killer hard enough to draw blood—and it wasn't Jimmy's blood."

Bill Hansen gripped my arm till it hurt. "But it had to be him. She was in the Seneca's sacred place! Jimmy was the only one of us kids who knew the way in there."

But Bill had to know. Bill had got to Mindy's body, hadn't he? Or had he taken her there and killed her himself? I looked at Bill Hansen. "Your family has lived in this town a long time, haven't they? Like for over thirty years? Back then, a lot of townies knew, didn't they?"

Hansen dropped my arm and stared as if dazed. "He told us to look in the sacred place. Said that Mindy was probably there with Jimmy. I followed the creek, went right at the stand of birches, and looked for the rock, then the maple with a hole through its trunk. He told me that we'd find them in the tall grass, where they take the girls. . . . Oh, God! We all saw her, with the arrow and the blood, but we couldn't go into that high grass, not with all those snakes crawling around." Shoving me backward, he crashed out the door. I followed, working through the crowd, looking for the red Santa suit.

"No point in shoving," a boy said. "Just go with the flow."

"You see the guy in the Santa suit? Hansen?"

He pointed to the stairs. I fought the crowd up to the main floor. "You see Bill Hansen?"

"Gym," a girl said. "Just saw him go in."

Two grim-faced men stood near the door of the gym.

"You can't go in there now, Miss," one said. I ran to the girls' locker room and dashed past the pool to the gym then stopped. Outside the door to the equipment room stood Lieutenant Jemison and Roger Sands. Behind them was Bill Hansen, still in the Santa Claus suit, his face not merry like Santa's but white and tense. His shoulders shook like he was crying.

"All right, sir, open the door and come out with your hands up," the lieutenant said. "Don't make us come in after you."

Sir? But why was I surprised? I knew, by now, that it couldn't be a kid but someone old enough to have hunted before the dam was built—Moshé Solomon! But what would

Moshé Solomon be doing in the gym equipment room? And why would Bill Hansen be standing there crying over him?

Suddenly, I knew it wasn't Moshé Solomon behind that door.

Moshé Solomon might have hunted up near Tonawanda Creek as a boy, but others had, too. And since the place had been off-limits to non-Indians ever since the dam was built, they wouldn't have known about the snakes. Moshé could have tried to run Paula down with the pickup, and he probably had a key to the BOCES garage since he was bringing cars there all the time. But would someone as religious as Moshé leave his house during the seven days of mourning? No way!

Yet with a good enough excuse, a faculty member could get a master key from the custodian, couldn't he? A master key would fit the photo lab as well as the BOCES garage door. . . .

"Okay, sir, we're coming in!" the lieutenant shouted, drawing his gun.

"No need, Jemison," Mr. Guthrie said. He opened the door and held out an envelope. "I was just finishing this."

"Why, coach? Why?" Bill Hansen cried, the tears streaming from his eyes now.

"Pray for me, Bill," Mr. Guthrie said. Then the policemen led him away.

chapter 21

"So Jimmy saw them?" my father asked.

"Yes, Dad, but not with his eyes. Jimmy sees with his ears, his friends say. He heard Mr. Guthrie saying to Mindy how much he loved her, and how when two people love each other, it's all right. But Mindy said she wouldn't, and she threatened to expose him. Then Mr. Guthrie gave her that line about how the school was a family, and how families kept their secrets to themselves. But Mindy would have none of it. Not even when he begged her to have pity on his children and his wife. Jimmy said that for just seconds, it sounded like there was a struggle. Then he heard something fall—followed by an eerie silence. He forgot about the snakes and moved through the foliage toward the sounds. That's when he saw Mindy lying on the ground and Mr. Guthrie a few feet back, his bow drawn. Jimmy cried out as Guthrie released the arrow. He said Guthrie turned and stared at him, then crashed away through the trees."

"And that's when Jimmy took off?"

"No. He looked at Mindy and saw this snake creeping toward her. So he picked up a rock and killed it. Then he stripped off his gloves and picked up her face scarf, which lay next to her head, to press against her stomach where she was bleeding. But as soon as he got up close, he saw her mouth open, with her tongue sticking out a little. Her eyes were open and staring, and he knew they were dead eyes. He covered her face with the scarf and left her."

"But if Mr. Guthrie had strangled her, why did he also shoot her with the arrow?"

"The lieutenant thinks Guthrie wanted to make it look like a hunting accident." I took a deep breath. "Mindy got killed because she refused to play by the rules. And Paula nearly got killed for shooting a picture—not of the killer in action as we'd thought, but her yearbook photo of the team. The time-stamp on the film was seven a.m.—the same time as the murder. Everyone was in the picture except Jimmy, Mindy, and the coach.

Dad sighed. "A young girl dead, and now

forty-one innocent Seneca wounded by a blast of dynamite. When will people learn that violence breeds more trouble?"

I couldn't answer that. Instead, I took a breath. "Speaking of dynamite, Dad. There's something else I'd like to talk to you about."

My father shook his head. "Another time, Vivi. You know I'm doing a Sabbath service tonight. There hasn't been one in this town for quite a while. Maybe with the new Hebrew school, the temple will come alive again."

"Oh, Dad, you did it then?"

My father nodded. "Two bright young seminary students were good enough to volunteer. They'll come down here on Wednesdays and Sundays."

"Dad, that's wonderful."

"Thank you, Vivi. But I spent so much time wrapping this up today that I barely have time to write my sermon."

"But Dad, maybe I can help you," I offered. "This week's Torah portion is on Abraham, isn't it?"

My father looked at me suspiciously. "Yes, it is. So?" Once again, I did some fast talking. When I finished, my father still looked doubtful. "You are sure, yakeerati? You researched well?"

"Yes, Dad," I assured him.

"Well, then," Dad stood up, "I suppose I have

a sermon to write now."

"You did call the service for eight, didn't you?" I asked, handing him his crutches.

"Yes. Now go to the phone and call Lieutenant Jemison. Tell him what you told me."

"I'll be there at eight," the lieutenant said, "and I'll station a few men outside."

"No rush," I said. "Our time is a lot like yours."

The lieutenant laughed. "When do you think you will start?"

"A little after nine," I told him.

chapter 22

Shirley Imber lit the two Sabbath candles and sang the blessing.

"*Ma tovu ohalecha Yacov,*" my father chanted.

"How goodly are your tents, O Jacob," some of the congregation repeated in English. Others—like Shirley, the Solomons, and me—spoke the Hebrew. The Solomon family's seven days of mourning weren't over, just interrupted by the Sabbath. On the Sabbath, even mourners were supposed to try to rejoice. The two little girls, Rifka and Hendel, waved to me. I smiled at them and their mother, whose husband and sons sat by themselves up front, their eyes glued to their prayer books.

"Are those the sons back from Israel?" Paula whispered.

I nodded and looked around. Compared to our temple in Buffalo, Temple Beth David was stark. The simple wood lectern was embossed with the words, "Hear O Israel, the Lord is God, the Lord is One." Behind the lectern, the commandments were etched on either side of the ark containing the Torah. No one would remove the Torah scroll tonight—this was done at Saturday morning services—but I knew that my father would speak on the Torah portion anyway. He always did, and tonight he had a special reason.

"This sanctuary is so beautiful," I whispered to Paula, "who'd ever believe that it's a hundred and fifty years old?"

"It isn't," she said. "A hundred and fifty years ago, this was the site of a Christian church. And long before that, it was probably a circle of stones where the Iroquois built a fire and prayed about the great tree and the turtle." She sighed. "If only I was living here back then!"

"You think that religion was better?"

"It was easier. That's for sure." She looked at me. "Do you know how a woman got a divorce?"

I shook my head.

"She put her husband's moccasins outside the longhouse. When he saw them there, he knew he couldn't come back in." Paula closed her eyes and I guessed she was thinking about her mother, who was sitting two rows in front of us. Every so often, Lee Ash leaned close to Shirley and whispered something. I tore my eyes from Lee's flaming hair and turned them on my father. Had he been looking at her?

"My heart sings for joy unto the living God," Dad sang. "One thing have I asked of the Lord, that will I seek after; that I may dwell in the house of the Lord all the days of my life, to behold the graciousness of the Lord, and to enter His sanctuary." Then his Hebrew intonations echoed above us all as he led us in *"Lekhah Dodi."*

"Come my beloved, with chorus of praise, Welcome bride Sabbath, the queen of the days."

Over dinner, I had asked him, "Do you think many people will come, Dad?"

He had put down his teacup. "If I didn't hold a service tonight, they would ask, 'What kind of rabbi is he?' Now that I'm having one, they'd have to think up good excuses for staying away. I think they will come tonight. Yes."

"What makes you so certain?"

My father had shrugged. "Aside from Seneca Bingo, I'm the only game in town."

Now, as we stood singing, I counted fifty-six, including the man near the aisle in the back row. In his brown suit, orange tie, and blue skullcap, he blended right into the crowd.

"What's Lieutenant Jemison doing here?" Paula whispered as we sat down again, but Dad was looking right at me. I couldn't answer. Paula didn't speak again until after the meditation.

"Blessed art Thou, O Lord our God and God of our fathers and mothers," Dad was saying, "God of Abraham and Sara—"

"Sara?" Paula asked. "None of our other rabbis ever said, 'Sara.'"

"God of Isaac and Rebecca—"

Shirley waved her hand. "Patrick, we never said 'Rebecca.' It's not in the book!"

"God of Jacob and Rachel and Leah," Dad said and looked at Lee Ash. "The great, mighty, revered, and most high God, Master of heaven and earth."

Paula grinned. "Well, what do you know? A rabbi for women's rights. I don't believe it!" She joined in the next round of prayers.

Rifka and Hendel were sleeping by the time my father started his sermon. "In last week's Torah portion," he began, "God tells Jacob to return to the land of his fathers.

"In this week's portion, we find Jacob making the journey back to his homeland. With him are his two wives, Rachel and Leah, and twelve children—eleven boys and a daughter, Dinah."

Dad smiled at the congregation. "If you've ever taken a family vacation, you have to know that getting this large group across the Jordan River—along with their goats, donkeys, camels, and cattle—was no small project." Some people laughed.

"Yet after he sees them safely across, Jacob returns to the other side of the river alone. The commentaries tell us that Jacob went back to retrieve some earthenware jars. But that would be like you or me going all the way back just for a plastic container."

"That would be the day," a man shouted.

"So," Dad said, "Maybe Jacob returns for another reason. Maybe he's not so sure that God gave him good advice and went back to be alone and mull it over. After all, he would have to travel through his brother's wild neighborhood. His children could come under a lot of bad influences there. Maybe get into trouble."

Dad paused, his eyes resting on Moshé Solomon. "So there's Jacob, alone on his side of the Jordan, wrestling with these problems and doubts. The Torah tells us he's wrestling with an angel, though some rabbis say he was wrestling with himself. Should he follow God's will or remain in a place he knows? Jacob comes away from the battle limping. But he's still alive.

"Whoever the adversary, be it an angel or

Jacob's own conscience, God wins. Jacob recrosses the Jordan River and joins his family, and God renames him Israel. From that time on, Israel will limp through life serving the Lord. But what of Israel's children? Would they trust in God as well?" Dad looked at Dov and Noah Solomon. Then, he turned back to his notes.

"Perhaps in fear for her safety, Jacob kept his daughter too isolated. Perhaps she was lonely for the company of other young women or just curious. The Torah doesn't give us the reason. It just tells us in Genesis XXXIV that Dinah, 'went out to see the daughters of the land.' And that, 'Shechem the son of Hamore the Hittite, the prince of the land saw her.' Did Shechem rape her? Or did Dinah go with Shechem willingly? Did he love her? It would seem so, for he asks his father to arrange for their marriage. Did Dinah love Shechem? We do not know. It would appear that nobody bothered to ask her.

"Hamore goes to Jacob with Shechem's request, but Jacob takes no part in the discussion. Whether a daughter's life wasn't important enough, or the father just couldn't deal with it, we don't know. Whatever the reason, Jacob leaves the marriage conditions up to his sons, Simeon and Levi." My father paused. "And we know what happened next."

As Dad moved on to the closing prayers, I

couldn't help looking at the Solomon family. Moshé was staring at his prayer book. Malka held her baby and her two little daughters close. But her eyes were on Dov and Noah, who were walking back toward the door. I fought the urge to turn around and watch.

"So what *did* happen next?" Paula whispered. "I've never heard the story before."

I glanced up at Dad, but he wasn't looking at me. His eyes were on Paula's mother. I sighed. "In the Torah, Jacob's two boys make a deal with Hamore," I said. "His son can have their sister if every male in his nation gets circumcised."

"Ouch!" Paula whispered. "His people agreed to that?"

I shrugged my shoulders. "I doubt if anyone asked them. Hamore wasn't running a democracy."

"Okay, so?"

"So a few days after Hamore's men were circumcised," I said, "when they were weak from the surgery, Jacob's two sons attacked them and wiped them out."

"Nice boys." Paula frowned. "Like the guys who tried to do in the Seneca when they were exhausted from dancing half the night."

"You got it," I said. The service had ended. I turned around. Jemison and the Solomon boys were gone. I knew that this time the brothers weren't going to Israel, but straight to the Pikes Landing Jail.

chapter 23

Two long tables covered in white cloths were laid out in the large hall in the basement. At the head of one table sat Shirley, a silver coffee service and a pile of cups in front of her. At the other end was a huge punch bowl. I headed for the second table, where the pastries were spread, my eye on a chocolate eclair.

People were talking, shaking my father's hand. Then the room got quiet as Dad did the blessing over the *hallah* (bread). Shirley picked up the coffee urn. Hands reached out for the goodies. One of them snapped up my chocolate eclair.

"Mmm, delicious," Rollie said, licking custard filling off his lips. "It was real nice of you guys to invite us in."

Paula laughed. "Well, since Jemison took care of the Solomon boys, there's no reason for you to be freezing your butts off outside."

"We really shouldn't be doing this, Rollie," Roger Sands said. "Our orders were to stay outside. Orders are orders while you're wearing the badge, even for a temp like you."

Rollie picked up a brownie. "In a minute, Rog. Meanwhile try this!" He turned to me. "Jemison said you helped him figure out who the dynamite twins were."

Roger Sands scowled. "Not that he couldn't have figured it out himself. Jemison is the best."

"Right," I said, "but this case was different from any he had before. Besides police procedure, it needed pilpul."

Roger screwed up his eyes. "What's that?"

I started to answer, but I was interrupted by Debbie coming up to us with a candy dish.

"Help me out, guys," she said. "My mom thinks it's a shame to waste it, and I'm on a diet."

I swallowed a couple of chocolate-covered raisins and turned to the deputy. "Pilpul is a kind of logic that Jewish sages used to understand the Torah. And people can use it to figure out other things, too, but only if they know the background. I remembered my dad saying how hard it was for the Solomon family to live here. They have to travel so far for kosher supplies and have to home-school their kids and stuff. And that got me thinking about why Mr. Solomon left Brooklyn to come back here after so many years. I doubted he returned just because he wasn't making a living in Brooklyn. A lot of Orthodox families are very poor, but they trust that God will take care of them. But what bothered me the most was how free Mindy was—getting out to football games and even hunting parties on the Sabbath. My dad would never allow that."

"So?" Rollie asked.

"So I called my friend Rachael for some help. She got on the Internet, then dug through all those old newspapers at our temple library. Ones we used for a 'prejudice and hate crimes' class."

Roger put down the brownie. "And?"

"She called me this afternoon. Sure enough, something happened in Brooklyn just before the Solomon family left. An Orthodox Jewish kid was killed on his way home from school."

"By Mr. Solomon's sons?"

I shook my head. "No, but he was a friend of theirs—a classmate. The Solomon boys were on a get-even team. They helped blow up a suspect's house. Four people injured. One dead."

"I hope the cops threw the book at them,"

Roger said.

"They did. At those they found, that is. But they never caught the Solomon boys. Mr. Solomon got his sons out of the United States before the firefighters had turned off the hose. According to the old news releases, it was a nasty explosion. And what do you think they used?"

Rollie reached for a cookie. "Don't tell me. Dynamite!"

"Right. Just like what they used at the Rocks. Stole it from a construction site."

"That's what made Jemison suspect them in the first place," Roger said. "We knew there was a ton of it at the construction site of Solomon's used car lot. But any of his workers could have got hold of it. It wasn't enough evidence to take the boys in. Your Dad's sermon made them think he knew. It didn't take much more to get them to confess."

"So that's why those creeps were at school in Israel?" Paula asked.

I nodded. "My dad thinks that Mr. Solomon moved the rest of the family up here because the Brooklyn crowd cold-shouldered them. Word gets around pretty quick. Orthodox groups in other places would probably have ostracized them, too."

"Poor Mindy." Paula sighed. "They just pull her up like a weed and dump her in the sticks. No wonder she went out to meet the daughters—"

"Whoa! That was Dinah," I said.

"Who's Dinah?" Rollie asked.

"It's a long story," I said and turned back to Paula. "I think Mindy probably just wanted to go to the high school instead of getting home-schooled with the little ones. She was probably lonely and wanted to be one of the crowd. The way I figure it, Mr. Solomon had no choice but to let her go. She knew what her brothers had done. If he didn't let her have her way, she could tell everything. Mr. Solomon couldn't let that happen. In Orthodox families, sons are most highly valued by their fathers. The sons are the ones who say the Kaddish, the prayer for the dead, after the parents are gone."

"So she was blackmailing him," Roger said.

Debbie frowned. "But if that's the case, why did she let him beat her up? She could have told about that."

"Oh, he wasn't the one who beat her," Roger said. "It was her mother. The lieutenant found that out, and he found out about the school sending Mindy to your house."

"How did he find out?" Debbie asked.

"It's his business," Roger told her. "He found out a lot of things, like it was Guthrie who fol-lowed Paula in the truck and trashed the photo lab to find that film. Jemison could tell during his questioning that Mr. Solomon didn't know beans about any beatings. The mother was something else. Under Jemison's questioning, she admitted that she suspected Mindy was dating non-Jewish boys. Whenever Mindy went out at night, Malka Solomon waited up for her with a belt."

"Mrs. Solomon admitted all that?" I asked.

"Yes. But even if she hadn't, we'd have known from Guthrie's confession note. He told how Mindy spilled her guts out to him about everything and sought him out to talk to him all the time. After the Bible meeting on Friday night, she showed him her bruises and cried. He said he only wanted to comfort her," the deputy sighed. "The next morning, Mindy was very upset. Guthrie remembered how tranquil the sacred place was and took her there. And when Mindy threatened to expose him, he lost it," Deputy Sands concluded.

"Just like she threatened her father she'd expose her brothers," Debbie sighed. "Poor Mindy. Do you think she loved Mr. Guthrie in her way?"

"Who knows?" Paula said. "No one ever asked her."

I nodded. "Just like Dinah."

"Who's Dinah?" Rollie asked again.

I looked toward the far table. My dad and Lee Ash were at the punch bowl.

"Ask my dad," I said. "I'm too thirsty to talk.

Let's go get some punch, you guys."

"Hi Mom. Hi Rabbi," Paula greeted them.

"*Shabbat Shalom*, Paula," Dad said and turned to her mother. "Lee, I'd like you to meet my daughter, Aviva. Vivi, this is Lee Ash."

"Hi. This is Deputy Sands and Temporary Deputy Hawkes. They stood guard all through the service, in case Lieutenant Jemison needed them."

"Thank you, gentlemen," my father said and shook their hands.

"Who's Dinah?" Rollie asked him. Dad put an arm around the temporary deputy's shoulder.

"Well," he said, walking him toward some chairs. "In our Torah, God tells Jacob to return to the land of his fathers. So—"

I poured myself a glass of punch.

april

chapter 24

Crocuses pushed through the leftover snow. A few winged migrants lighted on green-leafed branches. My grandma, the snowbird, had lighted, too, in time for Passover.

Mike took my hand as we walked up the path to the high school. "So this is where it all happened, eh?" I nodded and we pushed through the door. Nothing much had changed except the season. Kids coursed through school corridors like a new run of fish rushing through icy streams toward the spring holidays.

Mike and I went down to the basement. A sign on the bulletin board outside the art room said, "Easter egg hunt: Faith Church, Sycamore and North Creek, ten A.M., April third." Another one said, "Thanks to the Maple, April second, Hiawartha Rocks in the morning." In an empty space, I tacked up the sign we had brought, which read "Passover Seder, Temple Beth David, April second, sundown." Paula met us outside the door of the photo lab.

I hugged her and said, "Meet Micah Abramson. Mike, this is Paula Ash."

Paula nodded. "Glad to meet you," then turned back to me. "Come on, let's get the pollution mobile on the road."

The sky, which had been sunny, grew dark as we bumped along the snaking old foot trail, worn flat by Iroquois moccasins. Evergreens stood tall like royal guards above the queens of the state, sarsaparilla, trillium, buttercups, violets, and wild roses. Their sweet scents mingled with essence of spruce, pine, and hemlock.

"We're here!" Paula said.

I parked the minivan and we climbed out to a scene that sparked memories of another festival. Once again, the lot was packed with cars, trucks, minivans, and RVs. Children laughed and chased each other while their mothers cooked pungent food on gas grills and open fires. But men stood talking quietly. Every so often, they looked up the rocks and waved to the police officers on patrol.

"Come on," Paula said. "We have to pay our respects to the Wolf Matron. She'll let us into the longhouse."

Birds trilled. Two black squirrels scattered. A muskrat scurried across my path. Above the animal sounds, I heard drumbeats. We ran to the bark door of the longhouse. The Wolf Matron held out her hand. "Come stand next to me. We have touched the string of white wampum and confessed our sins. You're just in time for the speeches."

"Friends and relatives," the speaker began, "We are assembled to observe an ancient custom. It is an institution handed down to us by our forefathers. It was given to them by the Great Spirit. He has ever required of his people to return thanks to him for all blessings received."

I studied the man's deerskin kilt, leggings, and moccasins, all decorated with porcupine quills. His silver headband was decked with white feathers.

"The long feather at the back comes from the eagle," the Wolf Matron whispered.

"Friends and neighbors, continue to listen," said the speaker, "for the season when the maple tree yields its sweet waters has again returned. We are all thankful that it is so. We therefore expect all of you to join in our general thanksgiving to the maple and to the

Great Spirit who has wisely made this tree for the good of man. We hope that order and harmony will prevail."

The speaker's bare skin glistened above his beaded, braided belt. "Friends and relatives, we are gratified to see so many of you here. We thank the Great Spirit that he has been kind to so many of us in sparing our lives to participate again in the festivities of this season. *Na-ho*."

I looked at the Wolf Matron questioningly.

"It means, 'I have done'" she said.

"Na-ho," I repeated. It sounded so final. The Wolf Matron went to the hearth. It was her turn to speak next. She spoke about the duties of brotherhood. Other speakers followed.

"Na-ho," each said when he or she finished speaking.

"This is as bad as a Seder," Mike said. "How much longer before we eat?"

"Shush," Paula whispered. "It's time for the feather dance. There go Jimmy and Rollie." I watched the dancers take their places, their feathered headgear bobbing as they went. Of the twenty men, a few wore deerskin like Jimmy and Rollie. Others wore kilts and leggings made of various fabrics. Except for their armbands with the rattles and bells, they were nude from the waist up.

In the center of the room sat two singers with turtle shell rattles. "They're singing their thanks to the Great Spirit," said the Wolf Matron. As the singers shook their rattles and banged them against their seats, I tapped my foot to the beat. No matter how fast or slow that beat, the dancers stamped their feet to the rhythm, advancing around the room, their bodies erect and dignified.

"Look," Paula said, "they just changed places. Jimmy's the leader now." If Jimmy's eyes didn't work so well, his ears and feet made up for it. He didn't miss a beat as he stamped to the music. Every so often, he raised his foot and came down hard on his heel. The rest of the dancers followed his motions, except the women who had left their pots to join them. Moving to the end of the column, the ladies crossed it. Heel, toe, heel, toe, *heel!* They moved first to one side, then to the other. Then, suddenly, the music changed.

"The Fish Dance," the Wolf Matron said, looking at Mike. "Go join the men. Don't worry, your woman will find you." From all over the longhouse, girls came forward and chose their partners. I chose Mike. Toe, heel, toe, heel, we moved in two straight lines, forward, then back, forward, then back, never touching, feeling each others' touch nevertheless.

"The Planting Dance comes next," Paula said. "Then the War Dance and the Buffalo Dance."

"But when do we eat?" Mike asked.

Paula laughed. "After the Passing Dance. You'll love it. Each time the line moves, you get a new partner."

Mike drew me to him. "I don't want a new partner. I've spent most of the winter missing this one."

Paula winked at me. "All right then, I'll leave you two alone. I can get a ride back with Jimmy in Rollie's truck. See you at the Seder."

Up on the hill, smoke from the cooking fires misted the pudding stone rocks. Women stirred pots, turned spits, teasing our nostrils with scents of fried bread and venison. I took Mike's hand and led him from fire to fire, looking into each pot. Finally, I stopped. There were three kosher choices: corn, beans, or squash. But only the squash was kosher for the special dietary rules of Passover.

A basket of daisies brightened the table. On either side of it, silver candlesticks shone. In front of my father sat the Seder plate with the roasted egg, bitter herbs, parsley, and burnt shank bone. Also on the plate was the *haroset*, a mixture of chopped nuts, apples, cinnamon, and wine. It would remind us of the cement we used to set the stones of the pyramids we built, when we were slaves in Egypt. Next to the plate stood a decanter of wine, a pitcher of fresh water, and one filled with saltwater, a symbol of the tears we shed in bondage. On the other side of the table, three matzos rested inside the tiered doily my great-great-grandmother had embroidered. We had brought another family heirloom, too—a gold-trimmed crystal Elijah cup.

My father rose from the high feather pillow on his chair. "Welcome to our Seder," he said. "As we lift the first cup of wine, let us usher in the Festival of Passover, *Hag Ha Aviv*, the celebration of spring. Praised be Thou, O Lord our God, King of the Universe, who has kept us in life and sustained us, and enabled us to reach this season."

"Now what do we do?" asked Jimmy.

"Seder means order," I said. "We just follow it."

Paula nodded. "It's all laid out in the Haggadah." She pointed to the small book in front of him.

My grandmother smiled. "Every year, at this time, we read the story of Exodus, lest we forget. It's more than three thousand years old."

The Wolf Matron smiled. "One learns a lot from ancient tales."

"You're just lucky you're at tonight's Seder, Jimmy," Lee Ash told him. "Last night, Patrick made us read it in Hebrew."

"Is that the tradition?" Jemison asked.

"No," I said, "but it's faster."

Lee laughed.

Dad looked at us. "What's so funny?"

Lee and I exchanged glances. My father had seen a lot of Lee Ash in the past few months, and he seemed happier than he had been in a long while. Maybe that's why, in spite of myself, I had come to like her too.

"Our secret, Dad," I said, smiling.

"Why is this night different from all other nights?" Hendel Solomon, the youngest child present, asked.

We took turns telling her, reading from the Haggadah. After one of the pages, Rollie tapped my shoulder. "Blood, frogs, vermin, wild beasts, disease? Boils, hail, locusts? You guys have more weird baggage than we do!"

"Don't worry," Mike said, "We're not keeping score." He pressed my hand under the table. Two cups of wine later, Gram came in with a tray. "Who's ready for fish?"

"I'm ready for another cup of wine," Jemison answered, smiling.

Dad nodded. "It comes right after the blessing and the meal. Then we don't get another drop until dessert."

"That the law?" Jemison's smile faded.

"'Fraid so. We can't have the fourth cup until I'm ready to end the Seder."

"And he can't end the Seder until some kid finds the *afikoman,*" Lee said. "That's the matzo he hid at the beginning. Whoever finds it can sell it back for a price."

Rollie jumped up. "Not you," Shirley said. "You're too big. And anyway, we eat first." She smiled at Gram. "Tessie and I have been cooking for days."

We ate matzo ball soup and salad, chicken and meat, potatoes, spinach, and squash. Between courses, we sang. From the holy "Mighty Is He," to the comic "Only Kid," who was eaten by the cat, who was bitten by the dog, who was beaten by the stick, and so on and on until the Holy One inflicted the final punishment. My favorite was the number madrigal, which my father always saved for last.

"Who knows the answer to one?" his voice rang out.

"I know the answer to one," I sang. "One is our God, in heaven and on earth."

"Who knows the answer to two?"

"I know the answer to two. Two are Sinai's tablets. But one alone is our God in heaven and on earth," Mike replied in a strong tenor. And so it went, like a TV quiz show, until all thirteen were done. Then the little children set off on the great afikoman hunt. Rifka Solomon found it. Moshé and Malka smiled at her, and the little girl's eyes shone as she carried the matzo proudly to Dad's throne. After twenty minutes of bargaining, the small girl wound up with sixty-five cents. No one could say my father was a pushover.

Or was he? "Now run quick and open the door for Elijah," he said, and the little girl took off. As we welcomed the prophet to our table and fastened our eyes on his cup, I saw Dad's eyes move to Lee.

"Now is our Seder concluded," he said. "Each custom and law fulfilled. May we be worthy next year to celebrate a Seder again in freedom." At the words, "in freedom," he again looked at Lee, and the words sounded more like a promise than a plea. Gram nudged my arm and smiled at them.

I excused myself and walked outside. The night was cold and clear and lit with stars.

"What are you thinking?" Mike asked, coming up behind me.

I sighed. "I was thinking about those Passover nights before the divorce. Do you know how my parents taught me the 'Four Questions'?"

"Your father gave you candy each time you learned one. Two for the Hebrew. One for the English. Then your mother made you practice so you wouldn't embarrass her at the Seder."

"How did you know?" I spun around to face him.

Mike smiled. "My folks did the same thing. I hope some day you and I will teach our kids that way too." He took my hand and we looked up at the stars. *And we'll always be together, we'll always be a family,* I prayed.

Why does this Seder night have to be different from all our other Seder nights, I asked myself. But deep in my heart, I knew. For everything there was a season. My father and mother and I would never be a family again. It was time to relinquish my childish dream.

"Na-ho, Mom," I whispered. "Na-ho, Dad."